PULLING THREADS

Dylan Netter

Horizoncoaching.org

ISBN: 9798831633177
Imprint: Independently published

Cover design by: Art Painter
Library of Congress Control Number: 2018675309
Printed in the United States of America

*For my mom who had helped to foster the
man I am today. Thank you.*

We cannot solve our problems with the same thinking we used when we created them.

ALBERT EINSTEIN

CONTENTS

INTRODUCTION

Pulling Threads was written as a book to help readers read. It is a simple story in a familiar location. The sketch on the canvas is there. It is up to the reader to add the colors they see and fill in the picture as they imagine it.

This coming of age story takes place at Anzaldua University, a fictional school in the Northeast of the USA that was founded to help society understand borders and what they represent. The story centers around a Critical Thinking class at a Liberal Arts university where the students are taught to pull threads and see what unravels.

During the course of the story the characters find themselves in normal everyday situations and spend time working through them by building community and accepting each other as they are despite their differences.

We all wear different hats and lead double or triple or more lives. We are mothers or husbands or teachers or athletes or foreigners. We should learn to stop defining each other based on our differences and connect with each other more based on our similarities. We all want love and the freedom to be the best version of ourselves as we define it. Pulling Threads aims to be that story.

If you are interested in learning more about the author, Dylan can be contacted at horizoncoaching.org

PREFACE

At the core, I am an educator who believes that the job of an educator is to guide, to show not tell. Pulling Threads is just that. It's a simple book that provides the sketch or framework so that the reader can fill in the blanks and create a mental picture in their minds.

Pulling Threads tells the story of how students and educators work through the world of school and that not all life is doom and gloom. Sometimes our dreams are just around the corner or are waiting for the right moment.

All over the news, we are bombarded with bad news. From experience, after the storm there usually is a calm. Weathering the storm can be a challenge but all but one challenge we are designed to overcome and survive.

CHAPTER 1

Welcome to class. Please find a seat and make yourself comfortable. Anywhere. Choice is yours. Stand if you like. Sit on the floor if you please. You know you so you should know how you learn best.

I am the teacher for this class and congratulations on making it to your junior year. This is a two semester elective focusing on critical thinking and as I like to think, reading between the lines. My name is Professor Mark Styles. I hold a PhD in Philosophy with a minor in religious studies from my alma mater and soon to be yours, Anzaldua University. My thesis was about how Nepantla exists all around us, not just at physical borders. And as you know, Nepantla is the philosophy of the school's founder Gloria Anzaldua.

When I learned that Gloria had started a school, I knew I wanted to study here and to someday work here. I have now accomplished both. I am a self-described global citizen who has spent most of his life in some form of classroom from teaching windsurfing on the beach to middle school humanities in Denver to English around the globe including Africa and Myanmar to start.

A year is a long time to be together so there are some ground rules for us to have a productive and meaningful relationship. One, just because I am the teacher does not make me right. It, however, does not make me wrong either. Opinions connected to ethics are tricky. My right could be your wrong and vice versa. The real learning occurs when we find the third way that blows both of our opinions out of the water.

Most ideas and things as we will find out are opinion based. What's your favorite ice-cream? Mine is pistachio and I am sure someone in the class detests it. That is okay. We are here to explore through dialogue big ticket items like religion, race and sexuality and see what we can uncover. There is no wrong. What we are trying to explore and manipulate is the bigger question. Is there a right? So I will promise you this, if you are open to thinking, this will be an easy class.

Over the next two semesters we will try to uncover and deconstruct the building blocks of humanity and how it has been defined. Our purpose is to challenge the absolutes. Those who live in the world of I am right and therefore you are wrong. The rigid thinkers who want their opinions to be ours. We will be 'Pulling Threads' to see what unravels.

What I expect is simple. This is a junior elective class focused on providing those interested at a glimpse of mastery. If you are here, it is because you have chosen to be. If you find that asking questions about uncomfortable issues out there is not of your interest or like, I suggest switching to a different class.

Number two. You are all adults. I expect you to behave like one and to participate and complete your work on-time. I am sure you would be bothered if you went to a cafe, ordered a coffee and had to wait a week before you got the drink. Think of assignments as my coffee. I want to drink it when I am in the mood, not at your leisure.

Number 3. When we walk through the doors up there, we will put our differences aside and try our best to accept different points of view. This will challenge many of you as we begin. We are all built and conditioned and programmed. You. Me. Gloria

Anzaldua. Your parents. We are all just a culmination of our experiences. At least the parts we bring to the proverbial table. Ideas. We are here to learn how to hang up our rigidity and to put on our cloaks of malleability.

That's about it for the brass tacks of this class. Your syllabus is online and you may email me or stop by my office if you have any questions or concerns once you have perused it.

Now, with that out of the way, upwards and onwards as my father used to say.

When I was around your age, I spent a few months on the street as a punk rocker. Yes, I am balding now and yes, back then I had hair and yes, I had a mohawk."

The class let out a laugh.

"During those months, I was a member of a different world from the one I knew or had grown up in or belonged to. That experience opened my eyes to the scope of what is out there. It's not just one thing or another. Life is not usually black or white unless we are rigid in how we view the world. There are many shades of black and white and even more shades of grey.

That experience thrust me into a different culture. The one on the street. It is different from the one in houses and that differs from the one in apartment buildings. And today, we have many who live in tents and cars. Their culture is different too.

What that experience gave me, with knowledge of it, was the ability to be part of something I would have never known and to identify with that part of me when I need to. I am both an intellectual and someone who has felt the struggles of the poor and those literally just trying to survive. I have also spent time trying to help.

During that time it occurred to me that something was amiss. I was taught to believe that we are here to help our fellow man.

The Golden Rule. It was a rigid pillar of society or so I was told. Do unto others as they will have done to you. Be neighborly. What they don't teach is that 'others' and 'neighbors' are defined as "like you."

I was taught to cross the street and avoid the homeless and those who my parents feared. When I was homeless, I saw this from the other side. I would be hungry sitting outside a restaurant or on a corner and people would pass by like I didn't exist. When it was cold, some would sit outside clothing stores and again, patrons would pass by without a glance.

In those moments I realized there were opposing sides. The idea that we are supposed to help others but out of fear, the risk for many was too great if we did. Oppositional logic. Are we only supposed to help others when the mood fits us? Are the hungry really hungry? Do we really need shoes and coats to protect us from the weather? The answers are easy but it is also easier to talk than it is to act.

Most of us get swept up in our own pursuits of self-interest. Our parents and teachers and leaders of faith help us to attach our blinders so that we can succeed as individuals, adults and followers. And we ride that train without a moment of self-reflection until the moment that starts to unravel our thinking hits and the blinders that have been sewn onto our faces fall off. My moment was back then and 'Pulling Threads' is a class about helping you get to that moment without as much pain and anguish.

For some, the moment won't hit. It will always be cordoned off by rigid thinking and life choices that come from it. Their blinders are welded on with steel and unfortunately will stand the test of time. They will never really understand that their freedom has been enslaved by how they have been taught to think.

Many move on through life without ever having a thought that is owned by them. Their whole lives will have been built on the backs of the rigid conventions of others. How we view the poor. Religion. God. Education. Sex. Gender. Reading. Art. Love. What have you.

That is all for me.

"Any questions?" Styles asked.

"Are you saying that everything that is taught to us is a lie?" asked a curly haired brown-eyed young woman in the third row.

"No, but it is one of the questions to hold onto during this year. See what you uncover and revisit it at the end. What is left after you pull a thread and a pillar of yours suddenly dissolves? That's what we are here to do. Through dialogue, questions and answers, we will embark on trying to find the truth? And see if the truth can change over time? Or decide that the truth is just another opinion?"

"Bullshit!" snarled a young man in the back.

His name turned out to be Donald Abbot, the prom king and boy elected most likely to succeed. A handsome young man with an air of superiority.

"What is bullshit might I ask?" asked Styles.

"That truth changes. Truths are facts. Facts don't change," responded Donald.

"The night sky surely did and proves my point and questions yours. Would you like me to elaborate?" Styles explained.

"All ears."

"Questions and answers are the building blocks of thinking and therefore of humanity since we began. We are the only thinking creature with a known language and the ability to make and wield tools. Our survival was built on asking questions and developing answers. So what does this have to do with the night sky?

"I have the hope that someone has asked you to look up at the night sky or that you have discovered it on your own. It is beautiful and when you look up but what do you see sir?" Styles asked Donald.

"Stars and galaxies. That's what is there," Donald answered.

"And you. with the red shirt. Have you looked up at the night sky?"

"Of course. Especially in the summer. I even have an app on my phone to help me identify constellations.:

"And continue. What are constellations made of?"

"Are you joking?"

I shook my head no and gestured for her to answer the question.

"Stars."

"Stars? Would you agree Mr. 'Bullshit in the back'? I jest. I don't know your name."

"Yes," answered Donald. "I agree. The night sky is filled with stars and planets and satellites. That is the fact and what is there."

"And you, your name? Ms. I have an app on my phone."

"Sally," she stated. Sally Jones.

A hand connected to a curly haired red-head shot up. "So are you saying that is a lie?" she asked.

"No. I am suggesting that what we think is true may change over time," Styles stated.

Styles notices a boy in the back processing the idea. "You, young man. What's your name?"

"Charlie. Charlie Whittaker."

"You look like you were busy thinking."

"I don't see where you are going with this."

The red-head in the front agreed and spoke negating formality.

"Me neither. Rachel Weinstein is me. But the sky is the sky. It has been for all of time."

Styles was smiling inside but keeping his outer self composed. The class was off to a good start. Hands were up. Asides were being spoken. Thinking was being observed.

He walked to Rachel sitting in front of him and said two words. "Origin story."

Rachel blinked as she accepted the hint and then lost herself in thought for a few seconds and then raised her hand and answered when called upon.

"The prof is right," Rachel explained. "Facts and truths can change. The stars have always been there but what we saw and how we defined them has changed. The stars used to be holes in the layer between heaven and Earth. That's kinda cool when you think about it."

Some came around quickly while others took a few more moments to register what Rachel had said. Then there were a lot of nods, statements of agreement and a few who tried to still avoid the truth. Class had begun.

CHAPTER 2

Styles left class like he usually did. Reflecting on what was said and whether or not the class had been a success or not. Rigid opinions and debate on day one had always been a good omen from his experience. It meant the students were willing to fight and participate. It was his job to make sure that they could also think.

A student who asked questions was a student. A student who did not, became an automaton. Of course, balance was needed but students who asked questions tended to drive the class and their lives. They seemed to understand that their job was to supersede the teacher. Not stop at the equal sign. The more purposeful the questions, the further the student could go.

The whole Q & A process had always intrigued him. Asking questions and finding solutions was what separated man from animal. Yet, so many were willing to stand on their opinions as though they were solid pillars or facts. Most answers are not. If evolution has taught us anything, it has taught us that. Unfortunately, the big questions that man asks are not only the marrow that has tied us together, but also the disease that has broken us apart.

In his own college days Styles remembered one class above all others. Big Mountain, Scared Sky had been taught by Dr. Lopez if memory served him right. Lopez had taught Styles about questions and answers and evolution ultimately. That all peoples had asked the same questions and it was only the answers or labels that differed. Any middle schooler or older who had paid attention for a few minutes of their education has been told that different cultures had named the same entities just with different words. Zeus and Apollo. APhrodite and Venus. Cheese and fromage. God and Allah. Bread and tortillas. Same things. Different names. Much of modern day has been spent squabbling over definitions.

But that's where education stopped. Rarely was the bigger question asked: Why do we argue over the names of the same things that have just been labeled differently as language itself had been discovered and created? This question was rarely asked and was not automatically answered. Mostly, we were taught about the differences in a vacuum. As vocabulary to the answers on a quiz, not as an answer to the bigger questions that drive our lives. We have been trained to be disconnected from what we learn and not to see how it has affected our daily lives.

Dr. Lopez had taught Styles this and for that, he was eternally grateful. Lopez had taught him how to understand that the answers were a reflection of the questions that were being asked by both civilizations. Why were there floods? Neptune and Poseidon. Lighting? Zeus and Apollo. Hard milk? Cheese. Cooked wheat? bread. His job was to teach this to others.

Early civilizations had asked many 'whose to blame' questions. Who was to blame for the drought? A flood? A fire? A still born baby. Enter the gods into man's life.

Eventually, there were just too many deities to keep track of so it had become easier to define all answers under one, God with the uppercase G. And there are still remnants of times ago today. For example, in modern day sport, there are still remnants called a 'Hail Mary.' The last shot of the game that dictates the winner and loser. If the 'Hail Mary' succeeded, the game gets to take on the level of lore. Do you remember when? . . usually was the conversation starter to such moments. Whoever wins, gets to feel as though God were on their side. And this happens world over in all one in a million wins or fails.

CHAPTER 3

These ideas became the subject of Style's next lesson and after he introduced the topic, he was met with a few confusing stares and one hand eager to ask a question. He called on the student.

"How do we change things?" asked Charlie.

"By seeing things as they are, not how we want them to be," Styles answered.

"That's ambiguous," stated Rachel.

"I know and you have hit the nail on the head as to the topic of today's lesson."

Please be so kind as to hand this out. Rachel handed out a simple document titled 'Know Your Enemy.' A page with boxes to tick either yay or nay.

"I don't have any enemies. Everybody loves me," yelled a boy from the back.

Styles quieted the class down telling them to hold on to their thoughts for a minute.

"Some of these questions ask you to imagine or to think like someone you are not or a member of a group that you do not necessarily identify or belong to. The Romans were not the Greeks and that is what we are looking to explore. Why do we argue so aggressively over seemingly trivial manners?

"Let's get to work, shall we? Now remember this is not you. This is how you would vote if you aligned with a certain group.

1. Would you know how to vote if you are a person of extreme faith?
2. Would you know how to vote if gun ownership is a primary concern?
3. Would you know how to vote if you believe life begins at conception?
4. Would you know how to vote if you were truly worried about foreign invasion or war?
5. Would you know how to vote if you preferred Spring Break and Sturgis parties to the opera?

The class tallied their votes.

"By a raise of hands, and again, this is not a reflection of you, but of your ability to think. Who ticked 5 yays?"

Most of the hands went up.

"Okay. Next set. Are you ready?

1. Would you know how to vote if higher education including student loans are your primary concern?
2. Would you know how to vote if retirement is your big ticket issue?
3. Would you know how to vote if you were afraid of getting sick just because of the expense and bill?
4. Would you know how to vote if having the ability to find a secure job in your future was what you valued?
5. Would you know how to vote if you worry about food and shelter for you and/or others?

"By a raise of hands, and again this is not a reflection on you but of your ability to think critically. Who voted yay for 3 or more questions?"

Some hands were raised.

"Keep your hands up. Four or more."

Some hands went down.

"Five or more."

Zero hands left standing.

"What does this tell us? It's simple, really. We are programmed, starting from day one, to value certain ideals more than others. And that programming dictates who we are. Our identities in fact and what big groups we align like are we Jewish, Muslim or Chrustian? Democrat or Republican or other?

"Our enemy then becomes teachers who train us not to think for ourselves. Those who tell us what to do without concern for others but only concern for tradition or a cultural norm.

"I am going to paint with a broad stroke here. In 2006 actor Will Ferrel starred in a satire about Nascar called Talladega Nights, the Ballad of Ricky Bobby. The story is simple. Boy has a dream to be a racecar driver. Young man struggles to achieve his dream. Man achieves his dream. It is a funny film that I have watched many times. It was written as a satire and as factions have taken hold, has become a biopic of the American landscape. It clearly illustrated what happens when we are rigid thinkers against change, even the changes that are good for us.

"In the film, the main character is pressed to go back on an answer. Renege. He does not. This is happening while his foe is threatening to break Bobby's arm. It's an exchange in which the foe leaves many opportunities for Bobby to walk away. He chooses not to and has his arm broken in return. It illustrates the effect of rigid thinking. A person unwilling to adapt to a new situation like seatbelts, airbags, masks, helmets and other safety measures while being willing to pay and in the end paying the ultimate price."

"Where does that leave us?" asked Sally.

"Well, in a pickle really." You, in the first row. Please. "Let me ask, what do you see? What do you think? What is your opinion?"

"Well, I think it's about liberals vs conservatives and I am a liberal. I believe in education and in measures of austerity and helping others so I vote against the conservatives," replied the student.

The class could be heard agreeing.

"Okay. I can see that," answered Styles. "Now for the last set of questions for the day."

1. If you were a vegan, would you eat at a Steakhouse?
2. If you were a Muslim, would you eat at a rib joint?
3. If you were an Indian from India, would you eat at Burger King?
4. If you were a vegetarian and entered a vegetarian restaurant and were served chicken would you return it?
5. If you were a recovering alcoholic, would you frequent bars?

CHAPTER 4

Sitting at the plain table off to the right of center stage of the lecture hall sat Professor Styles. He had the habit of arriving early. He liked to watch the students filter in and see how they changed from the beginning of the semester to the end.

The lecture hall was normal. Seating for a 100 even though the roster counted only forty eight students in his class. It had stadium seating with a high ceiling and the colors were pastel erring on the side of being a little bland for Styles' taste. At center stage was a wood lectern with a microphone and behind him, a screen.

Styles sat and watched and made mental notes about the students. Who could he rely on to answer questions? Who did he have to worry about in class and out? Who was there to learn and who was there for an easy A? He knew his reputation as a grader. He focused on the three whose names he remembered from day one.

Charlie was diminutive in size but made up for it with a prickly personality, that as he aged Styles was sure would be described as salty. He was not to everyone's taste but his desire to help others was unlike anything Styles had seen before. In class, he would beeline after lectures to other students to check for their understanding and those who did not, he would find the time to help teach them. Intrinsically, Charlie understood that a team or a class was only as strong as its weakest link, and in this class, he found his passion and purpose, the ability to critically think.

Sally would have been called a teacher's pet if it hadn't been for her smile and beauty. Students and faculty alike gravitated towards her. They saw the spark of life that so few emanated and all wanted to be part of her story. She was the president of the student council and the school's top runner which is how she had landed at AU. She had been offered a full athletic scholarship to join the AU running team. She agreed only after making a fuss to allow her to pursue other activities while she studied. She had dreams of being a star athlete but knew that if she failed, she would need other skill sets to fall back on.

Rachel could only be described as an elitist punk bitch. She was off the charts smart and pretty in her own sort of way with curly brown hair but carried herself with an air of superiority that could almost be seen floating around her. She looked down on those around her that were not her equal. She could not accept them. She couldn't understand why so many seemed to succeed who deserved to fail. It went against her logic and her keen sense of fairness. She knew how others viewed her and in reality, didn't care. The truth was that most of the time she was bored around others.

Styles watched as Charlie, Rachel and Sally gravitated towards each other over the first few weeks of the semester. Most classes had strong students but many resigned to fade into the background only ever present for their grade with only one or two standouts. This year had three and for some reason, it made it better.

Having three students willing to argue made it so a consensus was needed to move on. Arguments have always been harder to end with only two sides unless it's a battle of might. Three means that the power structure shifts the moment an agreement is reached. It's the basis of democracy and fair voting.

If two are applying the same logic to a problem, it only makes sense to follow that thread of thinking to its end to see if it works. It was probably just an old teacher speculating for a moment but triangles are the strongest shape, because no matter what, two sides are always working together.

As Styles walked through campus, he would see each of the Triune as he liked to call them doing their thing. Charlie would be sitting with a coffee in hand and a confused looking classmate by his side. Sally with a flock of followers vying for her attention. And Rachel, alone with eyes darting left and right watching every person walk by as though on a search for her equal. It was why Styles was excited to assign the 'big assignment'. He wanted to know if gravity would do its thing.

Each year, on the second Friday of class, he assigned the 'big' project for the year which was responsible for the students' grade. It was quite simple. Each student or group of no more than four was to pick a theory and uncover the catalyst that created it. Math. Philosophy. Religion. Ethnic studies. The theory was theirs to choose.

What was happening at the time to make it possible? What was it a reaction to? And then explain it and connect it to the world and theories that define life as we know it today. And finally, make some educated guesses as to where we are going and what will be uncovered and what theories will shape us in the future. Like most open-ended learning, this type of assignment really allowed those who wanted to learn to dig as deep as they wanted to go.

After introducing the assignment and grading matrix, Styles opened up the class to questions and then allowed the class to get started by choosing partners and such.

Charlie made it happen. He saw it first, that this was a group assignment and he could choose his group. His eyes sparked as he searched the room for his peers. His eyes did not stop at the students Styles had seen him work with in the quad over coffee.

Rachel, Styles observed, was making a choice. Her eyes were focused straight looking at the wall behind Styles darting back and forth in thought. She was clearly indecisive weighing one option with the other. Would she work alone or pick someone to work with?

Sally was having the roughest go of the class. All those around her were vying for her attention to pick them. Sally had her head cocked to the side, ignoring her suitors and, what Styles assumed, formulating a plan to work either alone or with partners she would choose.

"You have the rest of class to pick your groups and brainstorm some ideas," Styles said. "I will leave you in peace. Good luck. This is a tough decision. It is for the year, remember."

And with that, Styles gave the class over to the students and watched.

Charlie walked down the center aisle of class and sat next to Rachel. "Hi. I am Charlie."

"I know. I heard you introduce yourself. What do you want?"

"The questions you ask are smart and the ideas you present pique my curiosity. I'd like to work with you or at least try."

Teacher secret. They see a lot and sometimes get to be flies on the wall. This was one of those moments. Styles was enjoying watching things unfold and thought Charlie's use of the word 'pique' correctly, piqued Rachel's attention. A smile creased his face. That would be a good pairing.

"Maybe. But I think we will have problems. You and I. We will get stuck. You are bright. I have listened but I don't agree with you a lot of the time. That will be a problem. What do you think?"

"Easy. We need a third person. I knew this before asking, but knew that without three equal minds, none of us would have fun. I'd wind up teaching the project. Not creating. Not learning. Not being challenged. That is why I came to you. I'd rather work alone than carry others. Help them for sure, but not do their work especially for a grade."

Rachel smiled. A rare site. "Who were you thinking for the third?"

"Sally."

"Good luck." Rachel smiled again and looked over and watched as Sally politely tried to ignore the advances of her fellow classmates. "You got it. I'll join if she joins."

The crowd around Sally was waiting to be picked as part of 'her' team. She smiled politely to all of them while formulating a plan of her own. She stopped and stared for just a brief moment, an extra second, on the two students sitting in the front row side by side and a smirk crossed her face.

Sally stood up. Gathered her things abruptly and started to walk down the aisle before being stopped.

"Excuse me, I'm Donald and was wondering if you would like to work together?"

Sally stopped for a second eying Donald before saying "No, I would not like to work with you. I suggest you find another partner. Good luck," and then continuing down the aisle taking the seat next to Rachel.

"I'm Sally. Nice to meet you. Rachel and Charlie, right?"

They both nodded yes.

"You two look like you are working together. Can I join your team?" Sally asked.

"Will we have to accept one of your fans in order to have you?" Rachel responded.

"No."

"Good. Let's get to work."

Charlie pulled a chair over and sat in front of the two women. The triune was complete much to the dismay of some of Sallie's followers who eagerly kept making passes by them trying to get their attention. The three ignored all as they got to know each other.

Of these passersby, Donald was. He was not the type of student used to being ignored by his peers. He did the ignoring. He didn't like the feeling on the other side of the coin.

Donald huffed off with his gaze on the group while noticing that the lecture hall had started to thin out. Some were leaving and some were sitting splattered here and there getting to know each other. Terry was the last student sitting. The only one Donald could see without a group.

"Guess it's just you and me, Terry," said Donald.

"Yep. Sounds good to me."

Styles had seen many students succeed and fail throughout his career. One of the student groupings that had always caused him reason for consternation were those kids who had peaked in high school and were now unable to capitalize on that success in university. He was talking about those students who never leave their hometown and can always be found at the local watering hole remembering the good old days while the world had passed them by. Their ability to think on their own was stifled by their desire to be popular and well-liked and the fact that their world was enabled to revolve around them. Donald was one.

CHAPTER 5

"So what do you think of Professor Styles?" asked Sally.

They were sitting in the second floor study room of the library overlooking the quad. It was a warm room with a mid-sized mahogany table, eight chairs, a small window in the door, a bay paned window looking out and at its center an old fashioned glass shaded lamp to give the room and the school the sense of academia. Above them was a popcorn ceiling with dull yellowed fluorescent lights.

Rachel sat with her back to the door. Sally sat to her right. Charlie sat with his back to the window. Their bags were on the empty chairs by their side and in front of them laid closed laptops, pencil cases and notebooks. Nothing was a strew. They were ready to begin.

"I like him. He's clever. I liked the question game and he didn't flinch when Donald yelled bullshit. He moved on like it was a normal part of the class. I thought that was cool," stated Charlie.

"Me too," said Rachel. "It was the first time I have been in a class in which the lesson doesn't seem canned. It felt organic like the lesson was coming from him in the now. Like he had talking points but nothing more. He was listening to us and using our responses to help teach us. I have never seen that before. Have you?"

"Yes, my running coach is similar. She focuses on giving immediate feedback that I can improve on and caters my training program to me. My strengths and weaknesses. She has me watch reels of me running and uses that as a guide. But in school, no, I have never felt like a teacher was listening to me. Cared, of course, but listened and ever present? No."

Rachel was antsy. She was uncomfortable in social situations that required small talk. It was a skillset that she had or cared to possess.

"Should we skip the pleasantries and dive right in or get to know each other first?" asked Rachel.

"Dive," said Charlie.

"Swim," laughed Sally.

Rachel beamed. She felt accepted and that she had found a home. OCD and organized to the max with probably a dab of Ausperger's thrown in kept her off the most loved list of most including her family. She liked school and learning and had a plan for her life, and at an early age, accepted that time was limited and to not waste it on trivialities.

Rachel should have been born to a different generation and on a different coast. Born in Santa Cruz, California, Rachel never embraced the surfer, yoga, 'life is good' movement that seemed to ooze from its residents. It wasn't until a trip to the East Coast to visit some distant relatives in Boston and New York that she ever felt accepted in a place.

"Mom. Dad. Someday I will live here," she repeated over and over on her trip. "This is awesome."

"Yes dear," her parents responded in placation. Happy that their daughter had found something that she liked but their interest stopped there.

Charlie was a thinker. Scratch that. Charlie was a questioner of everything. Who he wasn't was the type of person to ask questions to sound smart or to waste time. Instead, Charlie asked questions that sometimes frustrated both family and teachers alike because the answers took time to develop and were usually not simple and answered with either yes or no.

On the day Charlie's math teacher introduced the imperial system, Charlie was sent to the office, not because of his questions, but due to the response of anger and frustration and laughter it had generated from his classmates and teacher alike.

"America uses the Imperial system while other countries use the metric system. One is not better than the other. We just prefer the Imperial system," stated the teacher.

And then went on with his lesson explaining that 12 inches create a foot. Three feet create a yard. 5280 feet create a mile.

Charlie's hand shot up. The teacher told him to wait.

Charlie's teacher was a known car fanatic. He drove a 72 Barracuda. A perfect example of an American Muscle car.

His teacher continued, " So the imperial system is easy. It's based on the foot. A basketball hoop for example is ten feet. A football field is 100 yards. It's a simple system once you get used to it. You'll see."

Charlie wriggled in his seat sitting on his hands until his hand shot up once again. The teacher pointed and Charlie was told to wait another minute.
"Did you know that Denver, Colorado is called the mile high city because it is 5280 feet above sea level?" The teacher audibly sighed. "Are there any questions?" Charlie's hand darted up again. "Yes, Charlie. Ask away," the teacher sighed.

"Kill him dead but don't cry murder. Isn't that the basis of the metric system? Using kilo, hecta, deca, base, deci, centi and milli plus meter. That seems pretty simple. I read that in a book on math over the ages this past summer."

"So is the Imperial system, Charlie," the teacher responded with a hint of sarcasm.

Charlie spread his hands and said, "It doesn't make sense. We go from one foot, to three foot to 5280 feet. Make it make sense. The metric system goes from one meter to one decimeter to one hectometer to one kilometer by just adding a zero to the number. That's so simple. This Imperial system just seems complicated. Plus, isn't a foot the size of a shoe? And shoe sizes are different. Who gets to set the length of a foot?"

The class began to stir. Audible movement could be heard but no describable sounds.

"The foot is based on the size of the King of England at the time. We use his foot as the base of the Imperial system because he understood our need to have a uniform measure of length and weight across his empire which was the largest in the world at the time. It was a stroke of brilliance and stopped many petty arguments at markets over size and weight."

Charlie had always been a bit wily. You either liked him or didn't. It bothered him some but not much. He also always listened and when things were repeated often, whether stories, instructions, lessons or jokes, his brain would file the information and do its best at deciphering and organizing the data.

His father, Henry, was a printer and owned his own printing company. His family had been of some means and his father had had the good fortune of being sent abroad and studying for a semester in France where he met his future wife Geralydne.

Geralydne was smart as a whip with a pleasant demeanor and a keen sense of fairness and logic. She was a strong woman. As a child, she had been a gymnast on the bars. Spinning circles and leaping like a frog from mid air. She thought of gymnastics like she did all things, through shapes and order. Loop, loop, reverse loop, dash, spin, loop, loop, dash, line, land, Y. That is how she viewed the world.

Order was a value of hers and she could never come to understand the Imperial system of the British Empire and why America held steadfast to it.

One day when Charlie was about four, Geralydne was baking a plum cake. She was following a recipe out of the local paper. The recipe asked for a dash of salt. She took the time to define the unfamiliar word. She looked in the dictionary to find that a dash was equal to a pinch of salt. She went from D to P and found that pinch was what grandmother's worldwide are known for doing to the cheeks of their grandchildren.

Geraldyne added a pinch of salt, stirred the mix, baked the cake and was met by pursed lips and laughter at dessert time by Henry and Charlie.

Henry asked, "Did you add salt instead of sugar?" and then Henry and Charlie both burst into laughter until tears were flowing down their eyes.

Geralydne stood. Took the cake and the dessert plates in her hands and arms, walked into the living room, over to the fireplace and threw into it the cake, the platter and the plates. After she had composed herself, running her hands through her hair and ironing her apron with her palms she calmly walked back into the dining room.

Henry and Charlie had stopped laughing and sat waiting for what would come next.

"Henry. I need a new cake plate and a set of dessert plates. I was fond of the last set. Can you see if you can find a similar replacement?"

"After work tomorrow I would be glad to. Thank you for dinner."

And then Geraldyne turned her attention to her son.

"Charlie, I am French. I accept and love many things here in America. I will help you with whatever I can, but there are some things that the French do better, always. Cooking is one of those things. Now I know one of the reasons why. Our measurements are precise and based on logic, not whim or some Emperor's feet. The Imperial system is idiote and while you may need it for school, that is where your use of it will end. You will learn to use and think in the Metric system. Do you understand?"

"Yes."

Over the next few nights, Charlie was taught by his mother the metric system: how it worked and what made it more logical and efficient than the Imperial system. For one, it was based on using the same suffixes with different base prefixes like gram for weight, liter for liquid and meter for length. Not spoon, quarts and gallons.

So when the teacher started explaining the merits of the Imperial system it was hard for Charlie to sit still. His mind was racing because since the 'dessert incident', Charlie had uncovered many of the flaws.

Charlie responded to the teacher, "Ok, then why do we have metered parking instead of Imperial parking?"

The class laughed loudly.

"And why does your car have a speedometer instead of a 'speedofkingsfoot'?"

The class laughed louder and the teacher shook his head and grimaced. He had lost the class for the day and didn't want to be played the fool.

"Charlie, I think you know where you need to go," the teacher said while pointing out the door.

Charlie gathered his things and went to the principal's office where his mother was called. Geraldyne came promptly to pick Charlie up from school for the day. Apologized for the disruption Charlie had made in class. Listened to Charlie's story in the parking lot. Smiled broadly at her son and took him to the park for a picnic and to play outside for the rest of the day.

CHAPTER 6

The school year was in swing. Students had decided who they would work with. Styles only on occasion saw students opt to work solo. The last hints of summer were starting to fade and the first hues of fall were appearing.

"Again, this is not a class about teaching you what to think but as I like to think, a class dedicated to the Art of Thinking. Take for example our city. What is the defining feature of it?" Styles asked the class.

"You? Yes?" Styles pointed to a boy in a blue shirt.

"The university I guess or the tall buildings downtown."

"Both are correct and for different reasons. Let's explore the skyscraper," Styles responded.

The skyscraper at the turn of the 18th century was one of man's crowning achievements. It demonstrated his ability to wield tools and we had mastered the use of steel, cement and glass to create buildings that reached to the sky dwarfing the Cathedrals and other religious places of worship that had reigned tallest for eons. At the time, Skyscrapers were the creme ala creme of accomplishment and society would not be the same without them.

"Each skyscraper is its own city with multiple businesses and commerce and many employees from security guards to cleaners to handypersons. A skyscraper is a building of utility not of one-design. Even the tall apartment buildings are not of one design. The street level is usually inhabited by shops and cafes or restaurants. So not only do residents live there, but many make a living taking care of the building whether to keep it safe or to keep it clean or to keep it running.

"Now, the bigger question. Can something change from one thing to another thing?"

Hands shot up. The class was engaged and listening.

"Rhetorical questions," Styles continued. "Sorry if you want to answer. Again, your job as a student is not to agree or disagree with me but to uncover the reasoning behind your opinion so that you may defend it.

"If there is one speech pattern, I would like to eradicate it would be the lame answer. The 'I told you tos' and 'the because it is, I know it to be right' answers that we receive so often to questions. Unpack. Unravel. Pull threads. Explore. See what you find. I have my opinion and in fact, it may be wrong.

"Most of this class will be you working and me guiding. Think of today as me doing more of the latter. I want to show you how the thought process and the Art of Thinking works. Now, all over the world we celebrate the dead and their accomplishments. This is not debatable. We see it everywhere. From the plaque on the seat in front of you to the name of the lecture hall to the name of the school and out past the school to places like graveyards and museums. We can see the remnants of man's desire to be remembered after their time on Earth has ceased in geometric shapes. Little rectangles to big triangles.

"And we travel to many of these places snapping up photos in delight, many without thinking or making connections to the dead. The Pyramids in Egypt. The Hagia Sophia in Istanbul. Monte Alban in Oaxaca, Mexico. the Louvre in Paris, France.

Hussain II Mosque in Casablanca, Morocco. Angkor Wat in Cambodia. Athens, Greece. The Mall in Washington DC. These places we visit out of habit and tradition because they are all on the top ten lists of places to see, not out of reverence like we would if we visited a lost loved one at a cemetary to see their name etched in stone. The experience is different.

"But now you are thinking that I contradict myself. I said before that skyscrapers are teeming with life. They are the centers of commerce and of city life. I would agree. I contradict myself and do so with purpose and joy."

"Because!" Styles snapped his fingers and pointed in the air clicking the remote as an image of the pyramids appeared on the screen behind.

"What is the difference between this place and a skyscraper?" asked Styles. "How about you sir? Charlie, I think it is."

"That's a tomb for a pharaoh. Everyone in the class knows this. It's different from the Empire State Building. One has living people in it, the other does not."

"Okay," Styles stated clearly, giving it a pause before asking, "Why?"

"As you said. Cities are teeming with life. The pyramids are just relics of old, of history and some rich king's desire to have the biggest tomb or gravestone," said Charlie sardonically.

"I see that. So if I get the 'vibe' right in the room, who agrees with Charlie? The difference is one place is alive and the other dead for lack of a better term. That we are now living in cities and skyscrapers are monuments to our lives while the Pyramids are only relics of history and greedy dead men. Is that correct?"

The class laughed at the delivery and then proceeded to nod in agreement.

"Here is how I 'think'. This is what I want you to see. Imagine the pyramids being built. Human slaves or serfs, I assume, being told what to do and when to do it by some sort of managing class. The low man on the totem pole doing the heavy lifting while mid management drank tea and sought shade.

"Around the site I see tent cities much like those that I have seen worldwide that house refugees and immigrants. You have certainly seen it in the news. And where you have people, you have basic needs that need to be met or you no longer have people. The ruling has known this to be true throughout most of history and has applied this knowledge. Unhealthy sick slaves don't pick as much cotton or carry as much stone. We are not the strongest species on the planet. We only achieve our dominance by being able to manipulate tools and ideas.

"So here we are at the building site of the Pyramids. Huge blocks of rock are being moved to create the biggest and tallest mausoleums ever made. On top of that, they are located in a desert with little water.

"Were our basic needs different back then? No. We still required food, shelter, clothing and rest or we would die. And those who ruled us were keenly aware of the lines needed to maintain order and productivity. And the descendants of these workers or slaves accepted their lives much like a sheep accepts the herder as its protector despite the fact that at the end of its road, the herder will kill the sheep if it is maim, too wily or can't keep up. He sells the problematic ones to the butcher keeping the rest to reproduce, shern for wool and milk for milk and cheese. In other words, to be productive members of society.

"This has been going on for centuries. It begs the question of how slavery, not came to exist, but continued to exist since the slave populations has always outnumbered ten to one or more, the owner or ruling class. My theory is that it has to do with tools. Those who control the tools control the people.

"But back to the skyscraper. The Pyramid sites were teeming

with life. What I ask of you to discuss is what would happen if our modern day cities became uninhabited or barren of people? What would the skyscrapers represent? Imagine stumbling upon New York or Hong Kong or Paris without people. Without knowing what a skyscraper is, what would you think the tall buildings had represented or housed?

CHAPTER 7

"**A**aaaah!! Styles exhausts my brain. Why can't anything he says be simple?" Sally asked.

"Whewf." Rachel moaned. "It's like he sees the world through a different lens than everyone else. It's borderline insane."

"Or borderline genius," tossed in Charlie.

They laughed. Since being assigned the 'Big' project, Rachel, Charlie and Sally had started sitting together in class and meeting afterclass in the second floor study room of the library overlooking the quad.

Usually, they would leave and part ways with a casual response to the day's lesson. This was their new normal. Not even the suitors of Sally tried to interfere.

Each belonged somewhere on the spectrum with Rachel being farthest from center. She could only be described as a tech genius. While we see computers and screens and apps, she sees the code that created them much like a musician hears a symphony before it is written.

"Happy birthday! Rachel. You are almost a big girl," screeched her Grandma like grandmas do while pinching Rachel's then chubby cheeks.

"Go ahead. Blow out the candles, Rachel." said her mom while Dad cheered along.

Rachel blew out the five candles. One red. Two white. Two blue. Her parents had a patriotic streak running through them. Their home was painted white with blue trim and red shutters and on the porch flew a cleaned and pressed Old Glory during the day and ceremoniously removed before bed.

Their patriotism didn't change the fact that they lived in a trailer in a trailer park in a city filled with trailer parks within a city that could only be described as a manufacturing mecca. In some places, the flag is an exemption. There? The rule.

The good thing about the area was that it was relatively safe. Only those who worked and made a living supporting the area lived there. Kids still were able to bike to school and the fields at school were used long past school hours ended for pickup games of flag football and baseball and make-out sessions underneath the bleachers.

Rachel was the oddity. She preferred the library to the fields and only once made out with a boy underneath the bleachers to learn what all the hubbub was about. He kissed like an oyster. Wet with too much tongue.

In school, she was tolerated by her classmates but only with two, was she friends. Reggie and Irma. They were like her. More fascinated with tech than sunshine so it was no surprise when she received her first tablet on her birthday that she said thank you and immediately left the celebration to go understand it in her room.

She unpackaged the tablet carefully and read and analyzed the box and the instructions that came with it before turning it on and then went through the settings to find the coding files so that she could learn to decipher them. Within a year, she was coding and within two years she was able to sneak into the school's system with ease.

What Rachel lacked was normal everyday social skills often interpreting normal school banter as insults and going rapidly to fists. After the first few fist sessions, she received the crazy label and a wide berth,

"Hey Curly Cue," yelled the school bully from the grade above while leaning on a set of swings in the playground.

"Who? me?" Rachel asked.

"Yeah four eyes, you. What are you? Dumb?" The kids around her all laughed including her two friends Reggie and Irma. "Even your friends know I'm talking to you. You must be an idiot. Are you an idiot? Or just another wimpy girl?"

The boy walked over to Rachlel standing over her and kept spewing hate until finally he put a hand on Rachel. She ended it after that. She kicked him in the balls immediately following with a knee to the face. He collapsed to the floor.

Then she turned her 11 year old angst on Irma and Reggie walking straight up to them and said, "if you ever laugh at me again or someone being made fun of, we will no longer be friends. Do you understand?"

Irma and Reggie with gaped mouths nodded and said, "Yes."

From then on, Rachel was the leader of the pack and a force at school to be reckoned with or avoided. The pack left the playground and went on with their day as if nothing of interest had happened.

That was until the doorbell rang at 5:30pm in the middle of dinner. Her father Doug answered the door. He was met with a man of similar stature with a look of hate in his eyes.

"May I help you?" Doug asked.

"Apparently your daughter beat up my boy unprovoked at school today. She kicked him in the balls and kneed him in the face, breaking his nose. Then, she had the gaul to just saunter away like nothing had happened."

"Sorry to hear that. Kids can be wiley at that age."

"Well, what are you going to do about it? My boy was humiliated by a girl nonetheless."

"Not sure. This is news to me. This is the first time I've heard about it."

Rachel's father was the foreman at the textile factory that produced bedsheets and pillow cases. It was a good enough lot in life for him. It paid him well enough to live the life he wanted, which was one of modesty that provided him enough to put God, country and family first. He was gruff yet approachable, had a good sense of humor and his bullshit meter was off the charts.

"You could start by having your daughter apologize to me and then publicly apologize to my son at school. Help him regain some face. After all, he was beaten up by a girl."

Doug was a 'normal' guy in all respects who had a daughter instead of a son. This shifted how he saw the world. When Rachel came into his life, he didn't see the weaker sex as he had been taught, but the love of his life. And since then, he saw women as equals not inferior thus his collar was getting hot.

"Hold on, I'll be right back. As I said, this is my first time hearing about this. I want to hear my daughter's side of the story."

Doug closed the door in the stranger's face and went back into the house calling for his daughter to meet him at the landing of the stairs.

"Sit down," he barked.

She obeyed.

"There is a stranger at the door. He stated that you kicked his son in the crotch and then kneed him in the face before walking off like nothing had happened. Is this correct?"

"No."

"What do you mean? No."

"Why do I have to mean anything? You asked a question. I answered."

"Ok. Let me start again. There is a father of a boy at your school at the door who just told me that you hurt his son unprovoked. If that is the case, there will be consequences for you, but before I make a judgment, I want to hear your side of the story."

Rachel burst out crying. Sobbing. Doug watched in disbelief. This was a side of his daughter that he had not seen before.

Then Rachel composed herself, sat up straight and said, "The son of the man at the door is the school bully. He makes fun of those weaker than him all day everyday. Today, he chose to make fun of me which he does regularly. I ignore it. Then he touched me. I didn't like it so I kicked him in the balls and then kneed him in the face. He fell to the ground. The threat was over. I went on with my day."

Doug was having one of those parent moments in which his outward response did not mirror his inward one.

"You do understand that you hurt the boy?"

"Yes."

"Do you want to apologize to the boy?"

"No."

"Okay. Run off. I'll take care of it."

Rachel stood up and walked up the stairs to her room.

"Rachel. One more question. Why didn't you run away?"

"Dad, you taught me to stand up for myself and others when needed. Most of the time I ignore it. Today, when he touched me, I chose to fight." Rachel turned around and finished walking up stairs and disappearing from sight as Doug was left standing on the landing almost agape.

"Names Doug. My daughter is Rachel. Your son started it. She finished it. Best to teach your son not to start business he can't finish. It's a wise lesson to teach."

"What? Your daughter attacked my son."

"No, my daughter neutralized a threat. Your son laid a hand on my daughter. She responded in kind." Doug looked down at his wrist and then back at the man standing in his doorway. "In four minutes I will be out to take down the flag. If you are still within sight, I will take it as a threat and react in kind. Do I make myself clear?

The man nodded before having the door slammed in his face.

Doug's wife Judy was not a stranger to challenge. She had grown up on the rough side of the tracks and when Doug relayed the story, all she could do was smile.

"Guess tomorrow will be an interesting day which will include a call from the principal."

"I would assume," answered Doug.

"One thing that always gets me is how the bullied usually get in trouble for attacking the bully."

"No argument here."

"We should make sure that Rachel knows that we are on her side."

"She's not dumb. She knows. I love you and goodnight."

Rachel was back in her room chatting with Irma and Reggie

online.

"Can you believe his father came to my house?" Rachel asked.

"My dad would kill me," said Irma.

"I'd be mortified."

"Do you think you will get in trouble?" asked Irma.

Not sure. Mom and dad are chatting in their room. I guess I'll find out at breakfast.

"See you tomorrow unless you're dead. My grandma would kill me if I ever got into a fight at school," said Reggie.

That night Rachel did not sleep very well. Her mind raced as she imagined how the morning would unfold. Meekly she entered the kitchen.

"Morning mom."

"Morning dear. Did you sleep well?"

"Well enough. Hi dad."

"Hey. Morning. Could you refill the old coffee cup here?"

Rachel refilled his coffee, almost astonished. It wasn't until they were seated and eating breakfast that Judy tackled the elephant in the room.

"Rachel. We trust you to make good judgments. You are smart and much of your life will be spent on your own. We also know that if you are going to attack someone, it is for good reason. When the boy touched you, he crossed the line. We are proud of the way you handled the situation."

"Thanks," Rachel answered quietly, more to her breakfast than to her parents.

"But," Judy continued.

Rachel laughed, "I knew there would be a but."

"You are different from other kids. You know this. I know this. They know this. Pick your battles wisely and if you ever do have to go to blows, make sure you are the only one left standing. Do you understand?" asked Doug.

"Yes."

"Bullies exist. They will always be there. They thrive on reactions," said Judy. "My advice, learn how to walk through them as though they don't exist. They are not worth your time."

"Okay. Thanks mom. Love you dad. Have a good day."

Rachel grabbed her things to meet up with Irma and Reggie on their walk to school.

Reggie and Irma breathed a sigh of relief as Rachel exited the house. They had imagined that Rachel would be dead or grounded or something. What they were met with, confused both.

"Hey guys. Ready," Rachel said and headed for school without a care in the world.

Irma and Reggie gave each other a look of confusion and then hustled to catch up.

CHAPTER 8

Sally was different from Charlie and Rachel. She was one of the lucky. Those kids whose gift is identified early and then nurtured to success.

"All right kids. We are headed out to the field today to run your first lap on the track," the PE teacher said as the students bubbled with excitement.

"So let's check to make sure your shoes are tied. Great and now line up at the door," said the PE teacher.

The students lined up and headed out the door to the field. It was the first of September of first grade. They did their best to stay together and walk as a line as they headed out the door to the field and to the track.

The PE teacher with the help of her teacher's assistant lined the students up as best they could. Then she backed up about 40 meters so as not to impede their run while trying to keep them focused. When she was at the start line and her TA was off to the side, she said, "All right! Like we practiced in class. On your marks. Get set. Go."

Twenty first graders took off and within the first 10 meters, Sally was in the lead grinning from cheek to cheek.

The PE teacher watched in awe as this little girl distanced herself from her classmates and looked as though she was sprinting towards him. She looked down at her clipboard to remember the name of the girl. Sally she thought.

"Slow down Sally," he yelled.

"Why?" she yelled back and kept on trucking.

The PE teacher knew she would struggle in the second half of the lap returning her focus to the rest of the class before checking back in on speed racer.

"Go! Go! Go!" he exclaimed, almost forgetting the nineteen kids she had left in her wake.

When she showed no signs of slowing down in the second half of the lap and she could see Sally's grin still beaming, she made sure she had set her timer to keep track and clicked it again to stop it as Sally crossed the finish. She looked down in awe. 1:59 seconds as best she could tell. She wrote the time down and then continued to cheer the other kids as they finished choosing to run side by side, the student bringing up the rear.

"Good job kids," the PE teacher said at the finish line while many of the kids pretended to die while others pretended to be their favorite superhero with the exception of Sally. She just stood there. Smiling while observing the other kids and the coach observing her.

When class was dismissed and their primary teacher Ms. Rhodes picked them up to take them, Coach Eugene sat down at her desk and googled times for a 6 year old to run 400 meters and seeing was believing. His hunch had been right. Sally was only six seconds off of the best time she could find on her first try. Coach Eugene then called her principal with the exciting news.

Later that week Coach Eugene, her principal and Sally's parents, the Jones, Roger and Ellen, were sitting in the principal's conference room with Sally in between them.

"I have some news I would like to share about your daughter," said Coach Eugene. "Good news, I promise," he clarified.

"On Monday, we ran a lap at the track. Normal six year olds can complete the lap in somewhere between 3 and 6 minutes with others needing close to 10. Most of our students fall into the slower category with the exception of your daughter who on her first try ran an astonishing 1:36.

Roger and Ellen both sat slack-jawed, listening intently to the information. At home, it took a world event to get Sally off the couch so this was surprising information to say the least.

"As the PE teacher I would like your support, if Sally is interested, to focus her PE class on running. This would mean some days I would send her out to the track to run a workout while the other kids played basketball or badminton. I would need your consent to do this. That is why I called the meeting," Coach Eugene explained. "Your daughter has a gift that I would like to help nurture."

"Many students in our district have pullouts and special needs to match where the student is to their ability," added the principal. "Some need extra help and some need harder problems and we do our best to provide the extra help and support that is needed. Your daughter seems to be a gifted runner. It is not my forte but I put my trust in Coach Eugene's opinion."

"Would this mean she wouldn't play with the other kids?" asked Judy.

"Yes and no. It would mean that on non-running indoor PE days she would be responsible for the work with either myself or my teacher's assistant keeping track of her and keeping an eye on her."

"I'm not sure that is such a great idea," chimed in Roger. "I think Sally needs to be around her peers."

A fidgeting Sally breathing suddenly became noticeable in the room. All eyes were now on her and that is when a bright-eyed Sally pushed herself up off the seat and sat back down with her hands underneath her, visibly angry.

"Hello. Little person here. I am in the room. I am listening. Ask me?" Sally said as only a first grader can.

"Sorry Sally," said Coach Eugene.

"Excuse us, dear," said Judy. "You are right."

Roger raised a hand in the gesture of I understand and agreed before asking, "Well?"

"Thanks," she smiled and said, "I will run." And with that Sally's path as a runner was chosen.

From that day forward her life had been simple in the sense that she had purpose. By third grade Sally was training with the middle school cross country team and by 8th grade was racing for her future high school team as a rare phenomenon.

She was nicknamed very early on as Smiling Sally because once she started running, she started smiling from cheek to cheek and didn't stop until she was finished no matter the distance or the pain she was in. It was only after a run that she would allow the pain to kick in and smile to turn into a frown.

Like most student athletes, her success as a runner directly correlated to her success as a student. She thrived in school both in the classroom and out on the field. Again, she was one of the lucky few who found her gift early and had it nurtured and fostered by those around her towards success.

Sally's college life was no different. She was a runner for the collegiate team and was on track to qualify for the Olympics in two years' time. In the mornings, she would wake up early to do her workouts and then hit the books and class. Like many athletes and especially endurance athletes, she was a lone wolf which caused both boys and girls to hunt her.

CHAPTER 9

The Triune worked hard for that first semester and as fall came to an end winter took hold Sally made a request.

"All work and no play makes Johnny a dull boy," she stated one evening when they were together in the second floor study room of the library overlooking the quad.

"What do you mean?" asked Charlie.

"My running season wraps up this weekend at nationals and I have two weeks. I want to let my hair down. Go dancing. Get drunk."

"Sounds good to me. What were you thinking?" asked Rachel.

"I hear other students talking about a place called The Nest. They seem to make good cocktails and it's pretty cheap to attract the student crowd."

"I'm in," said Charlie. "Sure. Why not?"

Rachel was a bit more hesitant to say yes. She didn't enjoy big social events especially ones with loud music that made it difficult to speak but eventually she agreed.

When the night arrived, they met outside the main building and walked into town. Arriving at the club and waiting in line, Rachel finally voiced her displeasure.

"You know, we could go to the cocktail bar at the motel a few blocks down. I've been there once. It's quiet."

"What? Are you crazy?" asked Sally. "We are already here. After a drink or two and a dance or two, you'll be fine."

"Whatever you say," responded Racehl.

"By the way, I dig your shoe choice. Very practical."

Rachel, suddenly very aware of herself, looked down at her shoes almost ashamed. Traditional low top black and white Converse All-Stars. And then at Sally's matching all-white pair and laughed.

"Well. At least I know my feet will be at par with the prettiest girl in the bar."

All three laughed and the tension was broken and they were finally admitted into the bar.

"I'll get the first round," said Charlie. "Can you see if you can maybe grab that table over there? Gin and tonic for me. What about you?"

"A Mai Tai for me," said Sally.

"A what? Make it two? I'll have what Ms. Fancy drink is having too."

Charlie went to the bar while the two found a table and a place to perch for the night. As he walked back from the bar, it suddenly dawned on him that he was out for the night with two women, both beautiful in their own way. Sally was a knockout by any standard. That was easy to see. All eyes were on her no matter the room she entered. Rachel was wearing a sleeveless shirt, her hair was pulled back into pigtails, and he hadn't noticed even a hint of make-up but her skin tone was olive and alive. He suddenly felt like a lucky guy.

"I got three Mai Tais. I thought it would be easier to keep track of whose is whose," Charlie smirked as he put down the drinks.

They cheered. Clink. Clink. Clink. "To a night out!"

"Hey excuse me. I saw you from across the room and thought you might like to dance," asked a lanky guy in Nike's, skinny jeans and a Nietze T-shirt.

"Sure," Sally responded and got up to go dance. "Hey, come on. You two, too."

Rachel hesitated. Sally grabbed her hand and pulled her along and the four headed out to the dancefloor and whooped it up for a few songs and then returned to their table and drinks.

As they left the dance floor, Sally told the guy in the Nietze T-shirt, "Thanks for the dance. We'll take it from here."

The night went like that. The three drinking, a suitor arriving asking Sally to dance, the four dancing and the three returning to their table and more drinking.

The night waned. Then the last call was called, the light's flickered and the last song played. *Closing Time* by Semisonic. And the night was over.

"Man, I am feeling good," said Charlie. "I am not sure I want the party to stop?"

"The cocktail bar at the motel is open for another hour and they serve some snacks if memory serves," said Rachel with bright eyes.

They gathered their things, took the last sips of their drinks and headed out. As they passed a gas station and convenience store on the walk, Charlie excused himself for a few to go to take a piss.

"Can I ask a question?"

"You just did." Sally chuckled. "Of course."

"Why didn't you go for it with one of those guys?" asked Rachel. "They were all cute. That's for sure."

"I don't know. I think I came out to hang with you and Charlie. I wanted to see how our night would go. We work well together. I wanted to see the play side too."

"You and I are so different. As you saw, I don't have anyone coming on to me left and right let alone a line of good-looking guys."

Charlie returned and tripped, breaking the mood sending the bag of treats he couldn't resist flying at Rachel and Sally startling them. After helping him gather the assorted chips, candy and sweets, they headed to the motel bar.

Trying to save face for the flying food, "Three Mai Tais please." Charlie said to the barkeep.

"And french fries and mozzarella sticks please," added Rachel.

They waited for their drinks and food in silence. An awkward silence in fact with no one sure of where to start to keep the night going.

The drinks and food arrived and they toasted again and dug in, eating ravishingly the snacks and finishing their drinks as though they were now in a rush to go.

After they paid their bill and while they were getting ready to leave, Rachel asked, "Why didn't you hit on either of us tonight, Charlie?"

"I don't know. It would be too hard to choose between the two of you. Both are perfect in your own right."
And then they were back to awkward silence for a moment. Sally was the first to act.

Taking one hand of each, Sally said, "Maybe you don't need to choose after all." And then looked at Rachel who looked back and then moved forward. The two kissed and then Charlie was pulled into the embrace.

From there, the night went in slow motion.

"How about a room for the night?" asked Rachel when their kiss had ended.

In a slow motion instant, they went from three friends having a night on the town to something new.

They got a room at the motel and then they became a singular cacophony of limbs and sounds as they explored the parts of each other that they had yet to see.

In the morning, Charlie was the first to wake up. Sally stirred as he moved to get up.

"Can a girl get coffee in these parts?" she asked.

"Of course," he answered.

"A large black coffee for me."

Rachel's eyes opened. "Make that two."

CHAPTER 10

Rachel stirred as a door was open and closed as Charlie returned with coffee.

"Good morning," she said with a smile cheek to cheek replacing her normal stoic grin.

Rachel liked sex. It was something that she enjoyed doing. Sometimes with men who she equated to cab drivers. They drove to the destination and were in control but she could give directions as they went. A left there. Straight up there just a little more. Still a little more. A right turn here.

With women it was different. She felt like she was riding a tandem bike. Sometimes in front and sometimes in back but always pedaling. Slower. Faster. Faster yet. Keep that pace. Pull over. Let's switch.

So it was to her delight as she woke up to the world that the hand in hers was Sally's and Charlie was standing there with an outstretched hand offering her coffee. She squeezed the hand until it returned a squeeze back, sat up and received the coffee and gave the giver a kiss.

Sally was different. As an athlete she had grown up around lots of beautiful bodies, most willing to jump in the sack for a romp or two. She partook a few times but came to realize she wanted more. She wanted someone to wake up with who offered more than washboard abs and shaven legs. She wanted to think and to think about things other than sport. Especially other than running.

Sally loved running but was always bothered when she would hang out with her team or go on a date with another runner and the only topic of conversation that they could sustain during their off time together was running. She wanted more.

That was why, when a hand squeezed her and she awoke, she was delighted in the present moment. She had spent many a night going back to her dorm thinking about both Rachel and Charlie and wondering which she would choose if forced. She was happy to realize that the choice had been made for her and it was the answer not expected.

"Is there a coffee for me?" asked Sally.

"Of course."

Charlie handed Sally a coffee and again it was exchanged for a kiss.

After coffee, when they were done exploring and satisfying each other, they arose from under the covers, sweaty and smiling and ready for their day.

Charlie stood, walked to the bathroom, turned and said, "That convention question has been stumping me since Styles dropped it in class. Do you think conventions are hard-wired into us?" Closing the door behind him.

"He never stops thinking. Does he?" Rachel asked.

"No, he does not. It's his attraction."

"So it's not just me."

They both were giggling as Charlie emerged from the bathroom.

"Did I miss something?"

"No," responded Sally. "But we can work later if that is okay."

"Care to join us?" asked Rachel.

CHAPTER 11

"**A**nd for homework I would like you to explore the origins of slavery. More often than not, when we hear the word slavery, we turn our attention to the triangle trade between Africa, America and Europe and think only of how many Blacks came here. I would like for you to look past that to understand how slavery came to be. Why did one human decide that owning another human was okay?" Styles asked. "Where did slavery start and does it continue?"

Any questions was how Styles ended the class. The question was met with silence and crickets. Class was over and the Triune headed to the second floor study room of the library overlooking the quad.

"All right. The etymology of the word slave it is," Charlie said and they went to work.

Over the past few weeks, the Triune had organically created a pattern or system that worked for them. When they had an idea to ponder and explore, they started with teasing their brains online by setting a timer at an agreed interval of ten to thirty minutes, depending on the scope of the concept or idea, so that each would have time to explore the idea on their own before sharing with the others at the table.

"Twenty minutes," said Sally and set her phone with a timer in the middle of the table and the three opened their laptops and went to work.

When the alarm buzzed, they sat up, took a breather and started to discuss.

What they concluded was that in modern history, the USSR was a response by the Slav people to end their enslavement within Europe, and that within Feudalism, if you looked past the fairytale stories of King Arthur, Guinevere and Sir Lancelot, the serfs and peasants were slaves and the Knights, Vassals and Lords were tasked with the job of keeping them working to generate more wealth for the King exactly like a Southern white person on an antebellum cotton plantation or a warden on horseback overseeing a chain gang. The more history they explored, the more examples they found of those with wealth exploiting those without and came to accept that as the definition of slavery. When someone's life is controlled by someone else and examples of this in the modern day abound.

"Do you ever think like you are dumb? Like you miss the most obvious connections?" Charlie asked.

"No, I am brilliant. I know everything all the time." Rachel answered. "Shut up. Of course. That's the point. The old adage of the more you know, the more you realize you don't know. But I think I am starting to get what Styles is trying to teach us. He is asking us to question everything. The fascia that we assume to be true and that no one has asked us to think about before."

"Agreed. I have gotten this far by doing what I am told by my parents, teachers and coaches. I've never questioned the foundation that they are built on. I just assume and now believe that they have my best interest at heart. But what does that even mean? It's a fairytale concept. Most adults want the kids around them to succeed so that they can take some of the credit." stated Sally.

"It's like sometimes I am thinking something and then stop

the thought. I stop myself as though it's a bad thought because the daydream or something is about a taboo subject or not 'normative' and on top of that, feel a pang of guild. Do you ever feel that way?" asked Rachel.

"Yeah, for sure," said Charlie. "Our first night went against all things I have been taught about relationships and sex. When we left the hotel, my mind was spinning. Sometimes in spirals of sugary lollipops but other times into a dark abyss. We are taught not to question certain pillars like sex and marriage and family at a young age and because we don't, it's stifles our thinking during the period of our lives when we have the most time and need to think. In our childhood and even now we are uncovering who we are and who we want to be."

"It's like we are trained to believe we are free by those who teach us to live in a box," said Rachel.

"Yeah. We are taught to get in line and that being in line is positive and right and true, and that the kid out of line is negative and wrong and bad. Now that I see it, I wish I didn't," said Sally.

"Have you ever heard the story about thinking and Einstein?"

No said Rachel and Sally and then made a gesture to hand the floor, or table as it were, to Charlie.

CHAPTER 12

In middle school Charlie had an amazing history teacher, Mrs. Goodlow. All he could remember now about Goodlow was that she was a strong big Black woman who was known as the teacher throughout the school who was funny, fair and strict. She was beloved by all.

"Did you know that Albert Einstein walked every night and that during his walks he played brain games? Einstein took nightly walks and thought while he walked. Not about any specific topic but wherever his brain wanted to go. When I heard this, it shifted how I thought. Instead of forcing the topic, it allowed the topic to form and then I started to allow my brain to follow the thread instead.

"It was scary at first. Unbridling my brain. I had some 'crazy thoughts' but I think that was my brain lashing and fighting against the reins that had been attached to it by others. Once my thinking settled down, my ideas and thoughts started to become clearer and my ability to see more of the gray area greater.

"I started to understand and see just how branded everyone was in their thinking and how their thinking was a conditioned response to what was taught to them even though they believed it to be true. It was a hard lesson and I found myself suddenly alone regularly and thinking by connecting dots and observing others.

"In the summer between my junior and senior year in high school, I worked in a bike shop. It was a small locally owned business. It was fun. I shared a work stand with a boy named Garet who was religious and conservative, but we still had great conversations and what I thought was a solid rapport and maybe even a friendship.

"Hey Garet, want to grab a coffee after work sometime or meet up for a bike ride?"

"No man, I don't. I want you to know this," Garet said. "We are not friends. My religion and faith will not allow me to be friends with you. I enjoy our conversations here but we will never meet after work."

"That was a knock down wallop of a punch. It was honesty to the T, but when I broke it down, I realized it was indoctrination only. Garet had been programmed to think a certain way. It was clear as day to me. His Religion taught him exclusivity to only those who followed the same religion. That's not how humanity works or should work in my opinion. Humanity should ultimately be trying to figure out how to live together and prosper despite our differences and not allow our differences to guide us. It was a rough time for me and that is why I set my sights on NY and the East Coast. From what I could see, NY is still a place where all different types of people live on top of each other.

"So thinking like Einstein and being taught by Goodlow has led me here. And the truth is, it now looks pretty good," finished Charlie.

"Garet. What a dick! And waht a stupid religion!" said Rachel. "I think you are right. Styles is trying to get us to think freely. Get rid of the boxes and find our own shapes and ways. That is what draws me to you two. We do that here. We question everything and explore everything," she said, winking and smiling as sexy as someone who doesn't regard themselves as sexy.

They laughed.

"So back to the Slaves," Sally said refocusing them on work. "I found it really interesting to learn that Slaves were sold in markets in Africa. I guess I had expected Europe, even though not being taught it explicitly, that slaves were only an export of Africa controlled by Europeans, not a local product sold there in the markets as well to locals."

"So yeah, I get the thinking of the Einstein story and it's triggering right now all sorts of weird little paths and links to our collective human history," continued Sally. "To think that the root word of Slave is Slav and that represent the Slavics who now inhabit modern day Russia, the Ukranian and Polish region. It starts to make sense why the USSR formed. The Tsar Empires pre-USSR were probably created, like feudalism was taught to us, to protect the people within an area or region from not being stolen or taken and made into slaves. They would tend a field and give most of their yield to the Tsar for protection against slave traders who were searching for people's unprotected not realizing that they were still slaves just by a different name."

"Yeah. That makes sense," responded Charlie.

"And probably the Tsars, and probably the Kings too, did less beheading and more taking and trading when they felt a peasant was getting too big for their britches," Rachel interjected. "They understood that killing a producer didn't add to their wealth so they took more. Maybe that's the history of taxes. Create a system in which people are boxed into the area of free, and then told that to stay there, they would have to pay the very people who built the box."

"Wow. Yeah. It's like when we think about it, even the Aztecs, remember we were taught that they threw the slaves off of the pyramid. What if they didn't? Conspiracy theory here. What if they found a way to create the theater or illusion that they were, but in reality there were boats or slave traders waiting to take the ill-fated in exchange for more gold?" questioned Sally.

"It really makes you wonder if humans were so different 100, 200, 500, 1000+ years ago. Or have we always been the same. Viewing people below us, whoever that may be, as a product. We have value based on those who have created the system that defines value."

"The question then becomes when did humans start viewing other humans as a product or commodity to be sold and or exported. Did this happen out of thin air or was there a catalyst?" Rachel asked.

"Five minutes to ponder time," Charlie said and set his phone with a timer.

When the buzzer chirped, Charlie and Rachel could see that Sally had something to say. Floor is all yours.

CHAPTER 13

Sally's parents had been printers. They lived a modest life and Sally did not want for much. When her gift of running was discovered, her life got on a more even keel. Sure there were storms along the way, but when you have a destination in mind, it drives the work and the life doing it.

Sally remembered hearing stories about her Great Grandparents and Grandparents. They had had a small farm with some chickens, sheep and a cow or two plus some acreage of wheat and barley and corn. A typical western working class farm.

Sally's Greatgrandpa died of smallpox, like many during the period, but luckily he had sired four boys. All of whom built small homes on the farm and worked the land to earn enough profit to get by.

Until WWI, the farm worked smoothly. Then two boys were drafted and two boys enlisted. All for one and one for all was their thinking at the time. Only one came back. Soon after, the farm went to rot, the remaining boy, Sally's Grandfather, Arthur, and her Great Grandmother Anna moved to the city with what little they had left. Arthur met Lois and they married, giving birth to one child, Sally's mother.

Sally remembered hearing stories about the farm and the loss of it from her family and the others in the surrounding neighborhood growing up. Many had to leave their rural homes behind for lack of labor after WWI and WWII. It was commonplace. Replacing kin was almost impossible especially on a farm that yielded very little so attracted even fewer.

On one night, Sally could remember a conversation between Arthur and a friend of similar circumstance.

"I understand fighting for your country. I am a patriot and always will be. What I don't understand is why, after we win, we lose what we were fighting for in the first place?" Arthur questioned.

"I agree Arthur. It makes no sense. If we go to war and lose a hand, then that hand should be replaced by the loser. Your grandma had it the worst. She lost three hands. Seems like the least Uncle Sam could do would be to provide her with some prisoners of war to keep her farm going."

"A few slaves would have gone a long way, that's for sure," Arthur completed the thought.

Sally returned back to the group from her thoughts.

"It seems like slavery may have started as a means to replace loved ones who were lost during wars and battles to maintain businesses like farms and ranches. I had a Greatgrandmother who lost three out of her four sons in WWI after losing her husband to smallpox. They had all lived on a farm which she had to give up. She couldn't do all the work herself and couldn't afford to pay others to help."

"Sounds plausible," said Charlie.

"I even remember a conversation as such repeated over and over in the neighborhood I was raised in. That so many businesses had failed post WWI and WWII because of the lack of free labor, family workers who had a stake but didn't expect a salary," Sally stated.

"So maybe that's it. Slavery has always about labor and the

need for the hard work done cheap. Makes sense it would have to fruition to replace sons who had been lost during wars historically," Rachel pondered aloud.

They sat pondering for a few more minutes in the second floor study room of the library overlooking the quad and then called it a night and that was that.

CHAPTER 14

Professor Styles could see the light on in the second floor study room of the library overlooking the quad and decided tonight was the night to see if his presence would be welcomed. He crossed the quad, entered the library and headed up the center marble staircase to the second floor.

Styles was a teacher through and through. He lived modestly despite a small inheritance and some royalties from a few books and scripts he had written along the way. He didn't like high luxury, preferring function to form. Why would someone spend millions on things instead of millions to help others was a question that had bothered him for as long as he could remember. He had no answer.

On weekends, he helped to fund and work in a soup kitchen and taught two classes pro-bono: one, to adults in need of learning English and two, essay writing to students who needed practice and a guide. He had never married but did have a rescue dog who someone, probably a student graduating, had left tied to a tree outside the canteen at school one May. Styles had named it Lefty.

Styles looked through the door and could see the three students focused on their laptops with a phone in the middle of the table. He was not sure what to expect, but finding three students working diligently was always a pleasant surprise.

He left to go, then thought better of it and knocked on the

door. The three students jumped out of their skins. He smiled to himself. It must have been the first time they had company.

The three looked out to see Styles peering in through the rectangular window in the door. In unison they stood, beckoning him in and offering him the side of the table by the window that was free.

Styles entered, gladly accepting their offer and sat. "Sorry for the intrusion. It looked like you were all at task."

"Not a problem."

"No worries."

"Pleasure is ours."

"I have walked by many times and have seen the light on at all hours of the day and night. I wanted to stop by and see what you are up to."

Rachel was the first to speak. She explained how they had created the group for his class and had hit it off finding each other's company pleasant and they did better work together than separately no matter the subject. They had just gravitated from meeting once or twice a week to almost daily.

"Gotta study somewhere. This is as good of a spot as any. Plus, we have the view of the quad."

"So how is your project coming on exploring the origins of truth? Any thoughts or questions?"

"There is no truth," Charlie said.

Styles laughed and responded, "You may be onto something there. I think that is a thread worth exploring. What do you think of Rachel?"

"The truth is confusing because we all have our own truths. For example, I like rum raisin ice-cream and I know for a fact that

Sally doesn't. She hates it. Her truth is different than mine."

"And that's something simple," Sally chimed in. "If I had a dollar for everytime I was asked 'why do I run?' I'd be rich. It's the same idea. My truth is different from others."

"So when we are sitting here pondering, we land on just how challenging of a question it is," Charlie said.

"As it should be. Life is not easy unless you think very little which none of you do. I teach thinking. If you are challenged, then you are learning and I am succeeding. A double win."

"I just can't ever get the flat-round conundrum," Rachel stated.

"The idea that for most of humanities' history, the world was flat. That was the 'truth'. Then it was discovered and proved that the earth is a sphere or round. Start at A and eventually you will come back to A. That truth changed. And when that truth changed, all truths proven based on the earth being flat needed to be changed too. We think, somewhere, in the rewriting of the new truth, some big ticket items that needed to be adapted to the new discovery were missed or purposely omitted.

"That's what keeps us up at night and returning nightly to this room. We have some ideas but no clear answers," Rachel finished.

Styles bellowed and said, "I would not want to interfere with true thought. It would not be in your best interests. So all I will say is this. Carry on and ask me questions as the need arises." Styles rose from his seat with a smile and wink. "I bid you adieu. See you in class Wednesday and from the quad below I suspect tomorrow." And with that he left.

CHAPTER 15

Classroom rivalries rarely worked out well, either in the real world or academia was the thought Styles began his day with as he woke one morning in his small and modest home two blocks from campus. He had lived there for as long as he had worked at the university which had become a blur in his life. It was home.

For Styles, education had been a calling. A call to arms to be a warrior protecting truth and the ability to see it through the fog and muck. It was the only lesson he truly wanted his students to learn. To think for themselves. He had been an educator for the greater part of his life in one form or another. What he knew to be true, he had observed time and time again in classrooms all over the world, inside and out and between the rich and poor.

All sophomore years were a challenge for students. Sixth grade in middle school. Tenth grade in high school. Second year in college. It was the year that students chose their path. Students were no longer able to rely on their successes in school before. They were on their own without a crutch at the beginning of a long race. One that many failed. High school and college drop out rates were high. Students who succeeded had the ability to think for themselves and this is the tool Styles wanted to provide those who did not.

These were the years in which the successful students started to shine and the star student, who relied on the carrot to learn, started to fade. It was never fun to watch and intervening rarely, if ever, garnered results. Styles could see Donald as being one of these students.

Donald from moment one had thought of himself as the alpha. He was a winner. He was an athlete. He was the top of his class in middle school and high school. He was prom king. He was the dream boy and his parents only reinforced these ideals.

"Hey Dano," said William, Donald's dad across the video chat. "How are things at Uni going? Bet you are killing it in the classroom and out." Wink Wink.

"Stop, William. You are embarrassing him and me," replied Karen, Donald's mom. "But I bet you are too." Wink wink.

Donald had called his parents in search of support but also to find something that seemed to be missing that he was looking for but could not identify. It was the first time in his life that he could remember being unsure of himself. His grades were fine, women were still interested and he had made the Varsity baseball team as a second string outfielder. If the season went well, he would get to play.

But something was amiss. It was that dam class with Professor Styles. It was actually hard for him. It was forcing him to think on his own and he didn't like what was happening when he tried. He was also fully aware that if had partnered with one of the Triune, he could have relied on them to get the work done. But he hadn't. So he was stuck at the helm of his ship without experience or guidance of steering alone.

"So champ. Any chance you will play in Saturday's game?"

"No. Coach said that we need to first pull ahead in the conference for me to get off the bench or for Luke to get injured. Most likely later in the season but the spot is mine next year. Luke will graduate."

"We wouldn't want anything to happen to Luke this season, would we Champ?" William jested and the three laughed.

William, Karen and Donald were a family. One child. No siblings. All the attention and support went to him. With a few nods and handshakes behind the scenes just to help Dano along the way as 'good' parents do.

"Then we will meet you after the game and take you to dinner," exclaimed Karen. "Need to keep you strong and ready for next year when you do get play. Say 6:30 pm outside your building."

"Sounds good Mom," Donald said and they signed off. Maybe he would be able to broach a real conversation at dinner, he thought.

CHAPTER 16

Styles was sitting at the table in his kitchen sipping dark black coffee out of a smallish mug. He didn't like coffee mugs to be pitchers. The last sips were always too cool. He had tried espresso, and when in Europe, it was what he drank, but for some reason getting up and down from the table at home so often seemed like too much work.

So each morning he started his day with a small French Press of dark black coffee in a mug that could be filled twice. It was his ritual. That and ruminating about his students. This morning his wheel of students had landed on Donald. Styles had the suspicion that Donald would be in for a rough go between now and the end of the year. His 'teacher sense' was on high alert.

Maybe, Styles thought, he should change the name of the class. 'A Challenge to the History of Man.' He knew some students had picked the class thinking it would be an easy A. For some it was. For others, it was clearly not. They couldn't figure out how to climb the walls of the box they were stuck in. There is an art to thinking. It starts with a blank mind much like a painting starts with a blank canvas.

Education, he thought, was funny. Teachers spent most of their careers learning how to effectively communicate and teach each of the multiple types of personalities and learning types. Whether the teachers were keenly aware of it or not was a different story. Being aware takes reflection of which Styles had in spades and which some of his colleagues present and past did not.

Styles never questioned his sincerity or desire to teach students how to think. That was his goal. And he believed that it was the only lesson worth teaching. The ability to think got you to the finish line no matter the sport or activity. Thinking, to Styles, was simply the ability to solve problems.

Many disagreed with him believing that wealth and the ability to communicate collegially among peers were at the apex of education. That students who succeeded as adults were able to fall in line and follow orders and rules and because of this, they would succeed. He did not necessarily disagree. All games had rules that players needed to learn to reach the finish line or win. He just wasn't sure if the modern day finish lines were worthy sustainable goals and that all should be racing the same race.

And this is why many students found themselves knocking on his door to complain about their midterm grades. Each year, it was the same. Styles was unfair. Styles was not listening to them. Styles made them feel dumb. Styles was a bad teacher and their parents would have his job.

Styles finished his coffee, grabbed his bag, clipped on his helmet and rode his bicycle to school where he had an early meeting with his dean.

"Come in, Come in," said Dean Yoltas.

Styles walked in and smiled at the dean. They were friends or at the very least, had a mutual respect for each other.

Yoltas pressed a button on her phone and asked for two coffees to be brought to her office.

"So, nice to see you and I won't beat around the bush. Some of your students have complained that you are treating them unfairly."

"What a surprise?" Styles responded sarcastically.

"Are you?" Yoltas asked as though the question was required due to her position as dean.

"Possibly so, I would imagine. Life isn't fair as we both know," Styles said.

"Yes. I know. You know. Our budget doesn't know. From an educational point of view, there is nothing I want more than to send the students out of my office with their tails between their legs and an expulsion ticket in their hands."

"I hear a 'but' coming," Styles interrupted.

"But," Yoltas smiled. "My job is also to ensure matriculation, graduation and enrollment rates, not to teach fairness. Without students we have no money. Without money we have no jobs and the school fails."

"Ok. What do you suggest?"

Yoltas, always bothered when the solution had to come from her mouth, wanted to avoid culpability. She wanted to be able to pass the blame. She was too old to change and understood that her finish line was where she was sitting. She had prestige and a reasonable income. She also knew that with Styles, it was different. He understood this and the game she was playing.

"I think you should make your class pass or fail and only fail students of whom you have had multiple interventions which will include a meeting between you, the student and me," she said ready for a fight.

"Okay."

"Are you agreeing?" she asked.

"Yes."

"I thought you would argue the ethics or morality of the issue."

"No. You are my boss. If you want a ditch, I will dig it. I am your employee. I will do as I am told. Give all students passing grades. I do trust that if I look behind you that your hands have been tied professionally by someone above you which makes them above me. I can only rock the boat so far before it capsizes"

Styles had been in the same seat before. Principals and administrators believed in what they were doing. Providing failing students passing grades. It no longer bothered him. Life isn't fair and it would not be until money was not the dividing factor to success. He had learned this lesson early on.

CHAPTER 17

"**A**re you joking?" barked Donald. "You can't be serious. You are asking an impossible question."

"What makes it impossible? A student's inability to conceive an answer or that questions like this are rarely asked therefore making it a student's lack the experience in answering them or is it that you think some questions should not be asked?" retorted Styles.

It had become obvious that year that there were two sides in the class. Those that were eager to think and learn and who wanted the Triune as an ally and those that hated the Triune and in doing so stifled their ability to learn and think outside the box.

Like many teachers, Styles had offered a choice for the assignment. Students or groups needed to pick between one prompt or the other: One, create an origin story for God. Two, answer who defined God and why? Both asked the students to question what they had been taught about God and how those lessons helped to define themselves in the post Marvel superhero multiverse.

"What you are asking us to do is blasphemy," bellowed Andrew who immediately received a congratulatory nod from Donald.

"No, I am asking those of faith to define their faith in clearer terms if they have not already done so. And I am asking atheists and anyone else interested to assume that God was created by man and then answer the 'why'. Neither is blasphemous.

Styles had started to notice that the fabric of society was ripped or torn and needed mending. The fact that a rich man could walk by a homeless child or starving dog or cat and not feel a desire or obligation to act demonstrated his fear that society was on a precipice.

Empires rose and fell, but the constant had always been man's desire to succeed as a species. That seemed to be what was in the balance and at stake. The annihilation of the human species. The problem was not man's desire to accumulate infinite wealth. That was a different issue even though many clumped it into the same grouping.

Wealth accumulation, a quest for power, greed and want were all sides of the same dice. The willing destruction of the whole species was new to man and Styles struggled to put his finger on the cause.

Slavery, peasantry and indentured servitude were all synonyms for man's quest for power and wealth. Even though he wielded the ability to destroy what he owned, man rarely did. Usually man, even the rich man, protected his or her assets. Even though there were plenty of examples throughout history of leaders sacrificing their human property, Styles still believed they did so as a tool to maintain the power structure. To generate fear among those who were owned. Doing so for god, went against the code of the wealthy: to accumulate power and wealth and use it to accumulate more power and wealth.

So it was strange to Styles that society as whole was on a direct course for communal annihilation and was accepting it as a destination. No matter how much wealth and power you had, without air, water, food and tools, man would not have survived thus far. We are not cockroaches or ants. We perceive ourselves to be almighty and thrive in all corners of the world but that was not true. Roaches survive in all corners of the world as a roach. Humans survive by their ability to create and wield tools. Any person dropped off naked on either the pole or in the desert would certainly meet their end unless provided tools.

But humans seem to have forgotten their collective past with many believing that they are members of the strongest and fittest species on the planet. This is simply not true. When humans go extinct, many of Earth's species will still survive and thrive without man.

Styles had been all over the world and was an observer, a reporter of sorts. He saw. He saw joy and pain and success and failure everywhere. He saw it on strangers' faces and in newspaper images and in languages he could not begin to understand. Life was hard for many. Life was not hard for some. It worked out that way for some reason despite trying to tend their fields and do what was right.

As Styles aged, he came to realize that the problem and solution lived in the same place, in faith. Those who had faith and luck on their side, had easier lives than those who did not have either faith or luck. But somehow society seemed to attribute luck to faith. But so many were not lucky and were taught and then blamed for not having enough faith. They prayed more. Globally. Hindu. Christian. Muslim. Jew.

What those that lacked luck and faith, didn't realize, was that the lucky were the ones creating faith or at the very least, how man interprets God. With their accumulated wealth, they built churches, temples and mosques and around those churches, temples and mosques communities were built to protect the wealth of the lucky. Religion, as it is today, is based on a capitalist model. Before and after praying, we buy. Flowers. Incense. Prayer rugs. Bread, Coffee. Tea.

Go to any sacred place, present or past, you will find rows of sellers. They are the lucky owners. They no longer have to tend the sheep or the land. They just have to wait for sabbath. That's when they profit. What used to be farmland or the edge of the village has now been replaced with a temple to God. The lucky give thanks to God for their success, not the person who had the temple built.

Why was that? Styles often pondered. When the answer was clear but so many still arrived at a different solution down a different path.

"No, I am not questioning anyone's faith. I have faith. It is my own. Your choice to have it or not have it, as a sophomore in college, is up to you. What I am asking you to do is to define and understand, not your faith, but yourself and your relationship to it.

"We are all a culmination of the lessons we have learned. The stove is hot. All of us learn hot and stove separately. One as a noun and one as an adjective. Some need to learn the lesson by combining the two with personal experience.

Styles mimed, touched the stove, and then yelled, "Ow!" with many students jumping in their seats.

When the class settled again, he continued, "Many need to touch the stove to understand and answer "what is a hot stove?'. Yet many go through their whole lives without finding out the answer on their own. They accept 'hot stove' in good faith. This is a class on critical thinking. I am asking you to touch the stove and yes, it may leave a mark."

CHAPTER 18

"**F**uck!" Charlie explained as he threw his bag onto the table in the second story study room of the library overlooking the quad. "Sometimes I have no idea what Professor Styles is talking about."

Charlie sat with his head in his hands. Done. He believed he was at his outer limit of thinking. Questioning the existence of God seemed to go too far even for him.

Rachel finally broke the silence. "It's just a question that it's obvious it will garner an interesting debate if nothing else. The way I look at it, Style's is just trying to get us to imagine a different timeline, a new world. But that doesn't even work. Even in a new world, like Star Trek, God is still defined by man. I think he's just asking if we went wrong somewhere along the line."

Rachel stopped speaking. She had arrived at a thread or an idea. A thread that she knew would unravel parts unknown that she was not sure she was ready for.

Sally had been the first to the room today after class. She had yet to speak. She had taken her seat and focused on the unknown out the window. She too had an idea forming that was still in the grey. She was sure of it; she just couldn't see it.

Most nights they were able to get to work or just enjoy each other's company as they studied for other classes. Tonight was different. The connection was amiss. Rachel and Charlie were stuck. Something was there with them stopping forward progress. They were not their normal fluid selves.

Sally understood, and knew Rachel and Charlie well enough, to know that they were stuck in a loop. Each with his or her own past and definition of God unwilling to twist and apply pressure. It was not a safe place for growth. They had seen her there a few weeks ago when the topic of trans athletes in sports was brought to the table as fodder for conversation.

A trans athlete who was not allowed to compete in the Collegiate National Championships for Volleyball that year despite being short, even for a woman, testosterone levels within the designated range. At first, Sally had been okay with this. Then she saw past the facade.

Sally was a female athlete who had needed to prove herself and best most men in her middle and high schools so that she would be accepted as an athlete, not just a beautiful girl. Her schedule was set in stone and her mornings started early: rain, sleet, snow or sun. She had succeeded despite being seen by many just as a girl.

So Sally understood the marginalized component of the debate and felt for the trans athlete and knew how hard it would have been for that athlete to get to where he or she was. The obstacles that he or she would have had to endure to make it to 'a' starting line albeit, 'nationals.' But, that didn't change the fact that Sally still viewed a trans athlete as their birth gender.

Sally was also keenly aware that those who achieve top ranking success are forced to give up one thing or another in return. For many women, it was motherhood. For all, it was a balanced life. No top ranking elite athlete had arrived there by luck. They set a goal or purpose and went through hell and high water to arrive there.

So all those who reached the top were willing to give up something in return for their success. And whenever the trans debate hit the headlines, her first response was that the athlete was trading their gender for success. That their personal desire to be a successful athlete outweighed their connection with their birth sex. She thought this was relatively fair considering how many cut corners to achieve success.

It wasn't until Rachel chimed into the debate that Sally had found the thread that needed to be pulled and unraveled and found some of her pre-conceptions that were amiss.

CHAPTER 19

Rachel had always been the 'weird' kid or 'tomboy'. She identified with the marginalized, especially those with a limited capacity to think. She had realized at a very young age that she was different but also wickedly smart. Those who can see the trick aren't susceptible to it.

And this continued throughout her childhood. She was rarely picked on but when she was, it was not a bother. More, a mild inconvenience. However, when she saw others getting bullied, her sense of justice rarely lost out. Many bullies had had their academic or athletic prowess pulled out from underneath them without warning but always with evidence of wrongdoing. The stupid were caught with the bag of steroids or the answers written on their hands.

Harry, Rachel's best friend in middle school, was one of the first that she had stood up for. Harry, who later became Harriet, was a girl for all extensive purposes. But his parents were of the traditional belief that what was between your legs defined what was between your ears. His parents were unwilling to examine or even look at the thread.

Rachel, though, didn't need to pull it. She already knew that she stood out in ways that some liked and some didn't. Most of her classmates and those around her seemed to fit clearly into a box; she didn't. Labels galore. Boy. Girl. Football player. Cheerleader. Dancer. Athlete. Gamer. Nerd. Smart. Stupid. Rich. Poor. Black.

White. Asian. Latino. And then when you became an adult, the list just grew. Married. Single. Divorced. Parent. Chirstian. Jewish. Commuter. Business owner. White collar. Blue collar.

None of these labels interested Rachel in the least. All seemed boring and simple, but also designed for the boring and simple minded like Harry's parents. She did not resent them for being obtuse and rigid in their thinking; she did see them as a product of others with no ownership of self.

So when the day came while they were doing their math homework in 8th grade in which Harry told Rachel of his need to get through high school and turn 18 so that he could become her, Rachel had just smiled and said, "Great. Let me know if you need anything. Now, do you understand question 4? I'm stumped."

CHAPTER 20

Harry had thought it would have been a bigger deal for Rachel but saw that she had in the fraction of a second processed the new information, attached it to Harry as part of his identity, accepted the new Harry and moved on. It was the only time in Harriet's short life that she had felt accepted as herself.

A few years later while on therapy and pre-operation, she had met a man whom she believed would understand her despite what was still between her legs. He did not. He went into a blind rage and beat her to death and then jumped to his.

Rachel had heard the news from Harriet's parents the fall of her freshman year in college. About two years ago.

"The debate is not about sport. If you think it is, you are wrong," Rachel stated in a flat tone that neither Charlie or Sally had ever heard before.

She went on to tell them the life story of Harriet and then went on to explain how the transgender debate is just another debate between tradition and new.

Only in modern times has western humanity been so obsessed with gender and sexuality. If you go back to ancient times, it was more fluid. This is evident in the art of the times. Penises and breasts and orgies everywhere.

In Eastern humanity, the issue has only begun to rise due to the influence of western culture. Most Asian nations historically accept more than two genders with some nations like Indonesia viewing transgender as special or sacred.

The trans debate is not about sport, it's about modern tradition attaching itself to capitalism and being unwilling to take a look at the problem through the lens of finding a solution that is equitable for all players: male, female and trans.

CHAPTER 21

"**R**achel. Do you understand how much work female athletes have had to put in to compete, period? Just to make it to the start line. I am one of them. When I was young, it was not a problem. But once middle school hit, it was a struggle both on and off the field. Equality never comes easy. But sometimes I think all we are doing is trying to switch who is at the top of the pyramid."

"But solutions to problems are usually simple, contrary to popular belief. We talk about this all the time," rescinded Rachel. "Modify the system to allow for the new variable. Harriet and I would discuss this a lot. There needs to be a new team sport that allows all athletes to compete and a path to success. Like triple's tennis or team running or something. Where your success is based on your team and that team is a representation of all genders in society. Ten players: 5 men. 4 women. 1 trans. Or something like that. I haven't worked out the details."

"I see your point," said Sally.

"We are not all the same. If we were, we'd be Harry's mom and dad. Built by tradition to follow the leader. They missed the point of being parents. Loving unconditionally. Your parents didn't. They nurtured your passion."

"That I agree with," said Sally. "You are right and on to something. Breaking tradition. Girls playing football is ultimately the same issue. Where does it come from and why are there few traditions that include all humanity?"

"The only two I can think of are marriage and a celebration of puberty. Did you know that Buddhist boys and girls during that period have their heads shaved and go to a monastery for a week? Neat, huh." said Charlie.

"Maybe that is where we should dive. Into looking at what traditions were needed to create religion. I mean, I do think religion is different from faith and Styles is asking us only to explore the actual, not the mystical. What do you think?"

"Agreed," Charlie and Sally said.

"Say 15 minutes and then back at it?" Sally asked.

"We have a week. Let's ponder for a bit. I don't think I have the capacity for more work tonight," Rachel answered.

They agreed and packed up their bags and got ready to go.

"But I could use a movie night without the movie and getting a closer look at understanding gender relations," Rachel stated.

The three laughed while walking out of the library onto the quad in search of pizza and a movie night without the movie.

When they were fueled and then spent again, Charlie went for snacks and some beer.

With Charlie gone, Sally brushed back Rachel's hair from her eyes, "we will not agree on everything. You know. I think that's okay. We just need to agree to disagree and make sure that we hear each other's points of view."

Rachel smiled looking up at Sally and said, "Agree to disagree. Agreed. Just understand that I want you to see my point of view on this. It's important to me"

"I do," said Sally. "I think I need some time to process or tug at one of my threads. I am afraid of what I may find."

"What you may find is just a slightly different version and maybe one worth working towards. A system that's fairer to more. It'll never be perfect."

"Probably so. I'll try to take a look and see what I find."

"I mean like who knew we were polyamorous, but at least for now, we are," Rachel laughed before moving her mouth up Sally's leg until one was giving and the other receiving pleasure. again.

Charlie arrived back to his place to find the two women laying arm in arm. Did I miss anything he asked with a smile knowing that in the interludes of three sometimes there were trysts of desire between just two. They sat in bed drinking beer, snacking and decided on a film after all.

CHAPTER 22

Anzaldúa University Campus was centered around a quad where on sunny days one would find pick-up games of frisbee, small groups of students sitting, chatting on the grass and a few book readers leaning up against a tree. Surrounding the quad was the dean's house and office, the student union, the library, the theater and the main academic building standing at the North end of campus almost as a sentry reminding all in its view that the school was a place of learning. Outside of the gate one on each side, the Father of Logic, Aristotle and the Father of Reason, Descartes stood in marble.

The townies had a love-hate relationship with the school. They loved it during football, baseball and basketball seasons. Like many schools, a large portion of the budget was earned by the athletic department with ticket sales, merchandising or donations from alumni, and on game weekends, the village thrived. Hotels, inns, B&Bs and most restaurants including the brand names were by reservation only.

AU was founded by Gabriela Santiago who had been born on the Texas Mexico border in 1941 where she had spent her formidable years. She had worked hard in the classroom, harder on the softball pitch and even harder in the fields. She had graduated at the top of her class with a full ride scholarship to University of Santa Cruz where she had discovered Gloria Anzaldúa and had been taken under her wing as a mentee.

Anzaldúa was an American scholar and philosopher whose theory about the borderlands resonated so much within Santiago that she had dedicated her life to it. The theory was simple: those born on borders live simultaneous dual lives. They were neither one group or the other, but both at the same time, being able to move in and out of each culture and into the other with fluidity, much like someone who is multinational and bi-lingual. Their identity and tongue is not developed by one but by both.

Santiago knew this to be true and she was able to put to rest the idea in her mind that she had a split personality. She had recognized early on that depending on which side of the border she was on, and with whom, would dictate automatically some of her responses. When she first heard Anzaldúa speak, the stars aligned and she came to understand herself with clarity.

This clarity led her to success as a business woman on the Texas Mexican border. She opened up a restaurant which quickly became a chain that was two-sided. One specializing in authentic Mexican food and the other in American Tex-Mex. With her success and fortune, she decided to build a tribute to Anzaldúa. One that would help others find and accept their identities and put the voices in their heads to rest.

Sadly, Anzaldúa had passed away before breaking ground but had said in one of her last conversations with Santiago, "the world moves from East to West. That is the direction of the sun and the moon. I have recognized in my life that big changes in society head from East to West too. The problem is finding the border where West ends and East begins.

Santiago stated, "As much as I hate to admit it, I think you are right. I agree even though I know many would not. Most beginnings start in the east and move west so will start in the east and then grow."

And that became the mission statement of the school that was etched into the rock of the stone gate: Many beginnings start in the East and then move West. Start here and then Gow West to Bring Change.

The school attracted many different types of students. Many were athletes and athletic scholarships were doled out in abundance to top performers, especially young women whose grades equaled their performance.

Other students came because of the prestige. In the 15 years since AU was founded, its alumni had followed the mission leaving in its wake, success stories that circumnavigated the globe from East to West arriving back East again. Some of the biggest new companies had been founded by AU alumni and AU alumni like to hire new AU graduates for the basic reason that they understood themselves in relation to others. AU grads young and old knew at their core that they would have to wear many different hats at the same time to succeed.

And some just threw the dart at the board and where it landed is where they went. Sally was the athlete having been offered a full-ride scholarship for her running. Rachel had researched schools, landed on the AU homepage and after reading the mission statement had only applied there. Charlie was the latter. He had been accepted to a few schools, was on the fence about going, and rolled a die to pick. It had landed on AU.

CHAPTER 23

The Triune were not an island to themselves. The three were popular in their own right. They just preferred each other's company to those around them most of the time. One of the exceptions was Iris.She was a second generation Japanese American, valedictorian of her high school class and voted most likely to rock the world.

"Why do you spend so much time studying with Charlie and Sally?" Iris asked Rachel. "You know many people talk about the three of you as the weird group in the library."

"No, Really?" Rachel said. "I'll make sure to take it into consideration or Not!" She laughed.

"And why are you spending so much time studying for Professor Styles's class. It's only an elective. Even if you get a B, what will it matter?"

This was a question that the three had been asked since the beginning of school. One that showed how few students went to school to learn. They just wanted the degree. The Triune did not. They not only wanted to think; they thrived on it.

"Why? Easy. I like learning how to think. Today, for example, Styles asked us to ponder the Wizard of Oz as a metaphor for capitalism. I mean, he said just think about it. Then he set a timer on the board and sat as the class discussed the question fervently."

Styles had arrived to class that day looking like he normally did, about three weeks too far past a haircut on the hair that was remaining, and a little flush and sweaty from his commute from a brisk walk across campus or run right before class. He was wearing his normal: running sneakers, dark khakis, a button down shirt and a worn sport coat. Today, it was his brown tweed. He rarely wore a tie.

"Good morning class. I know it is early for some of you and for others, you are raring to go. Class today will be a discussion based on the 1939 film *The Wizard of Oz.* I assume most of you are familiar with it since there were only 12 of you at the school theater showing last thursday. Those who are not missed, too bad and so sad."

Rustling papers and the opening of backpacks could be heard in the hall along with some groans and oops and audible whews. Week 7 had clearly stated in bold, Homework for Week 8 - watch the Wizard of Oz - Free showing in Santiago Theater 7Pm Thursday October 11th.

"It seems many of you are not prepared for class. Those who are not, may leave. Those who are not interested in today's discussion, may leave. I'll give you two minutes to decide."

After bags had been packed and only the interested students remained, Styles got down to business.

"When we pull threads, we have to be willing to accept what we find. Many have asked the question, 'Is WoZ a metaphor or is it just a film?' I will give you the answer. Yes. Your opinion is yours like your views on faith. I am not here to challenge you. I am here to give you tools to challenge yourself.

"Once a reader or audience member sees past the third wall. Past the screen and the story and thinks there is something more that meets the eyes, there is. Something organic takes shape and exists even if the reader is unsure or unclear of the meaning.

"Let me give you an easy example. I hold before you a plain blue capped Bic pen. Steven, here, examine the pen. Is there anything fancy or different about this pen that the millions of others that you have seen."

"No sir," Steven answered.

"Next question. Steven, is that pen you are holding a piece of Art?"

The class laughed as did Steven as he cheerfully stated, "No, it's just a plain blue pen."

"Then why is it on display at the Museum of Modern Art in New York City as an example of modern art in the industrial design section? The Bic Crystal is a work of art but until the question was uttered, it was just a pen."

"This thing. Cool. I'm keeping yours," Steven responded. "I'll ebay it for millions. Thanks Prof. I have really learned something today. To pay attention and finders keepers, losers weepers."

The class laughed as did Styles.

"My point is simple. Once we ask 'is this art?', the object becomes art. Now, let me be clear, there is a world of difference between good and bad art. That is where the difference lies.

"So back to WoZ. There are many theories about what Baum was trying to teach us, or what metaphors can be uncovered when exploring the story. If it is asked about, the metaphor has been seen at least by one set of eyes. Me, I would like you to apply the metaphor of Capitalism and American exceptionalism and see what you uncover. Class is over at 10:30am. It is now 9:45, as you may be guessing, get to work."

As the timer ticked time away some students were at square one trying to find summaries online of WoZ while others were toiling away deep in thought or discussion.

"So it is obvious that Oz is Wall Street. The wealthy behind the scenes calling the shots," stated Charlie.

"And the munchkins are the working class doing what they are told out of fear," said Rachel.

"Then the witches are law enforcement, creating a fear based society that has to believe that the yellow brick road leads to success," Sally said. "And maybe the road is a metaphor for a river of gold and all society believes they have equal access to it since they walk on it daily."

"That's cool," Charlie said.

"Agreed." Then Rachel asked, "But what about the poor? Do you think the Munchkins represent the poor and middle class?"

"Good question."

They were stuck with time ticking away.

"I'm going to see if Styles will give us a hint. Be right back. Try to figure out Dorothy and the 'other' Triune," Rachel said with a laugh and walked away.

Styles was a teacher, who believed questions by students were where the learning happened. He stated this frequently and therefore usually had a line of somewhat patient students waiting to ask him questions in the classroom and out. He never bored or tired of this part of his job.

After a few minutes, Rachel stepped up to his desk and explained what the Triune had uncovered. And that they were stumped on who represented the largest group in society, the poor.

"And that my dear is the question that needs to be asked, and I will answer it with a question that may point you and your friends to the answer. Did the poor matter to Baum in 1939?"

Rachel had found that one of the differences between High School and College was that most teachers wanted students to think more broadly. In High School, many of the teachers had been kids themselves. No more than a few years older than Rachel who were just looking for a piece of the pie. A normal life in a normal city doing a normal job while giving back to society the best way they could. But one didn't become an English Teacher in small town USA if you were the best of the best. They landed in bigger cities in prestigious high ranking schools or didn't study education in the first place. Those with higher capacities shot the moon while those who were limited, tried to survive. College was different. Styles was better. Plain and simple.

Rachel was stunned as an answer formulated while she went back to the group. She didn't like the conclusions she was drawing but couldn't find another solution.

She sat back down with the group and said, "In 1939, the poor couldn't afford or understand much so Baum didn't see them as valued players in society. He didn't write them in because he didn't believe they needed to exist. We are talking about TV and film which by design are exclusive," Rachel stated. "Much like today. A billion poor people could die today and no one would care collectively. One old celebrity dies and we all mourn for weeks. Baum wanted the poor to identify with the characters even though they are not represented."

"Makes sense. The poor matter very little and in a capitalist model, matter even less. Capitalists view the poor as leeches with nothing to offer except an occasional breakout success story but even those are becoming rarer. Capitalists only value consumers, who spend. Not those that squeak out a life," said Charlie.

"That's dour but true," agreed Sally. "Which brings us to the Tinman, Lion, Scarecrow, Dorothy and Toto."

By the time class had ended most everyone had agreed that the witches represented the two party system. Oz was the donor class behind the scenes. The munchkins, the working class. Dorothy, everyperson which included Toto. And that the 'Other' Triune represented recreational activities designed to stop the everyperson from seeking the truth.

The brainless Scarecrow represented addiction to drugs and alcohol, wanting society to be inebriated or without the ability to think.

The heartless Tinman represented the working class's willingness to work until they couldn't work anymore with the idea that before they rusted out and were broken, they would become rich.

The courageless lion was humanities collective fear. Our lack of desire to see things as they are, opting to see things through the lens of meekness and an unwillingness to change instead.

CHAPTER 24

Donald and Terry sat at an off-campus watering hole drinking beers.

"What the hell is Styles talking about? Oz is Wall Street. Man is Dead. Who does he think he is? Nietzsche?" Donald spoke aloud to his audience of one.

Terry responded, "I don't know. I don't really care. All I know is that we still have to get the project done. I need this A."

"Yeah, yeah. I know. But I have half a mind to find out if the Dean really knows what's happening at her school?"

Donald and Terry were opposites. Donald had been an A student in high school where learning seemed to come easy with only one exception.

He had an old school English teacher, Mr. Ritter, who had asked, as an essay question on an exam, 'what do you want out of life?'. Donald had written what he had expected would get him an A. Instead, at the top of the exam there had been two words he had never seen before, 'See me'.

Donald knocked on Mr. Ritter's door during lunch.

"Come in, Donald. Take a seat," Ritter said. "Did you bring your exam with you?"

"Yes," answered Donald as he rifled through his knapsack to find it, finding it and handing it to Ritter.

"Let me see what we have here. Hmm. Hmm Huh. MM. Hmm. Yep. Just what I thought I remembered."

Donald hadn't written about his life. He had written about the life of an automaton. It was as generic and as stock an answer as an answer can be. There were words on the page but the words meant nothing. It was as if he was repeating back to himself all the things others had told him he wanted: a good paying job, a family, a nice car, a big house, money in the bank.

"Donald," Ritter started. "Is this really what you want from life?"

"Of course it is," Donald responded. "And it answers the question. So why did you take off 25 points?"

"Did you read the rubric? And use it like a guide for content like I asked?"

"Yes."

Ritter realized he was in a deadened conversation unless he shifted tactics quickly.

"Okay. Describe your future home?"

"Huh?"

"Describe your future home? The one you wrote about."

"Sure. Like I wrote. It's big and white with blue trim and shutters with a few trees and white picket fence around the yard. Oh yeah, and in the driveway there is a basketball hoop."

"That is an accurate description of millions of homes. What you were expected to answer as it says here," Ritter flipped the pages to the rubric, "To describe your life as you imagine it will be. Make sure your examples are clear and well thought out. Not stock answers."

"I don't understand. What do you mean?"

Donald didn't like Ritter. He was too much of an old school hippie for him. He wore jeans and cowboy boots to class everyday and what was left of his hair was pulled back in a ponytail. He always seemed a bit unkempt and he taught that poetry and making connections and figurative language was and would be important to his future. Donald saw Ritter as a fool.

"Here is an example?" Ritter said.

Donald nodded to get it over.

Ritter continued, "When I retire, I would like to get away from cities, small and big. I would like to live in a home walking distance to a market and either the beach or mountains. Other than that, I am pretty open to the actual home. I would just like it to be small enough so that my wife and I don't have to spend a lot of time cleaning it and big enough so that we have enough space to do our own thing. It's specific, not fabricated. I can explain in more detail if you wish."

"No. I will rewrite it like you want."

Ritter had known that when he had circled the 75 on the page that it would come back to him. Students like Donald were in school to get grades, not to learn. Worse yet, students like Donald had parents that supported this methodology of learning and would fight tooth and nail to ensure their child's academic success. Learning was secondary. School was about the number or letter next to the name.

Ritter did not like the Donalds of the world. He viewed them as entitled brats who thought they could one up the teacher, if need be, by crying foul to mom and dad. Every year, Ritter had taught at least one student like this whose parents would come in to raise hell to fix their child's problems. These experiences lead Ritter to using ironclad rubrics.

"I would be glad to allow you to rewrite the essay. The rubric states and, as I have explained it to the class, you may only receive credit to boost your grade by one letter. In this case, you have a C. The best you can boost it to is a B. That was made very clear."

Donald nodded yes and left the office thinking he would still have the last laugh. He rewrote the essay and had still only received a B instead of a C after using his parents as a weapon against Ritter.

Donald had gone home, complained to his mom and dad about the unfair treatment he had received from Ritter. They had called the school and complained to Principal Santos that Ritter was being unfair to Donald and that she had to do something about it. After the call, Santos went to find Ritter.

Santos had been in this situation many times before. Irate parents claiming to have sway with the district and screaming for heads to roll. She was also a principal who would try her best to stay on the side of the teacher during witch hunts, but had learned her lesson long ago to first talk to the teacher.

In her first year, Santos had not spoken with the teacher first and had blindly supported him against a raging parent. It turned out that the teacher had made a mistake and therefore so had Santos. So from that moment on, she started at the source with a quick investigation.

"Ritter, am I interrupting?"

"No. Come in. I am guessing this is about Donald."

"The Abbotts just called. Are you sure?" Santos asked almost rhetorically.

"Yes. The parents called and yelled at me for quite some time about how you are the worst teacher in the school and that learning poetry and figurative language is a waste of time and that your head will roll."

"That sounds about right and what I had expected. Donald made a few mistakes in the first part of the exam but missed the topic clearly in part II. The essay. The rubric was clear. He, like some others, dive in without reading the instructions, even after I repeat during class over and over and during the exam to read all the instructions."

"Just needed to be sure. Thanks and have a good day. We'll weather the storm together."

The storm never came. The Abbotts were all bluster. Donald rewrote the essay but never really learned the lesson. It was why he was so frustrated with Styles. It was a class with no wrong answers, but as he was finding out, clearly there were better answers and certainly dumb ones.

"I just don't understand how to think like a crazy person. The idea that movies and TV shows are being used as propaganda is down right idiotic. Thinking that the billionaires are at fault for not helping others to survive is dumb. Survival of the fittest. And guess where we are, the top of the food chain," Donald pontificated to his audience of one.

Truth was, most things were over Terry's head. He was the model of a model general American. He was taught to do but not to think too hard by all of those around him. Weekends were devoted to sport and church and weeks were devoted to school and church. He had graduated high school easily, primarily due to his devotion to church as the principal was also his pastor.

What Terry was finding out in college was that he didn't like to think. He dreamed of getting his degree so that he could go back to his home town and become a minister, living out his life among those who believed in the same God and who thought the same way about how things should be. That creationism was real and evolution fake.

Behind the thin veils between Donald and Terry, was a fake friendship between two young men who had a disdain for the other but knew that without each other, they would have no one. Neither was willing to break the facade. Neither was willing to change. Neither was willing to learn. Their alliance was built on their beliefs that they were right and that others were wrong.

"Yeah. Styles is blasphemous. He would be run out of my town and for good reason," Terry stated.

"Sounds so good to me," Donald responded while taking a long pull from his beer.

"Cheers to Styles getting his due," Terry toasted as they clinked their bottles knowing that no action would ever be taken. One was too afraid of God and the other too afraid of himself.

CHAPTER 25

Over the last few years of teaching Styles had come to introduce the question of God to his students just before they would leave for holiday break. He had come to realize that the 'God' topic was a challenge even for the best students and he liked that the issue would simmer while they were away. Both the most devout and the atheists needed the extra time to let their opinions brew.

"Good morning and welcome to class. Today will be our last class before winter break. I wish you all safe travels. Now, let us get to work.

"Today is a bit different than normal. As you know, my modus operandi is to usually drop big ideas and let you stew about them before coming back to center to find a consensus by guiding and sometimes being a referee in the class."

Styles made boxing gestures and some of the students laughed. Others were waiting for the assignment and itching to get on with their vacation.

"God. For you Star Trek fans, the final frontier. No teacher or class that is designed to help students think better does not broach the subject of God. Now, I know that some of you are ardent believers and others are atheists. Both still need to understand God if we are to ever have a healthy society. Believing in God is not what is being questioned." Styles gestured to the class. "All we will ever have is the now and the now exists here on Earth. Since Earth and time are both constructs of man, doesn't that beg the question whether or not if how we interpret has been constructed God too?

Hands were raised. Those hands were quieted by Styles patting his hand to the floor.

"Today, just listen. A month from now we will discuss and argue and debate this issue I am sure but today, just listen." Styles continued, "So here are some observations to think about God in a different light. Connect God to other things and see if you can find what holds your idea together. What connections can you make? God and sound. God and prayers. God and the universe. God and football. God and math. God and love. God and life. Your assignment is to write out some answers. Journal. Blurb. Diary. Paragraph. Poem. Just think and write about how God is connected to your life and your life is connected to God. Atheists too. Just because you don't eat meat doesn't mean that the meat industry doesn't have an affect on your life. Good luck and safe travels."

The students shuffled out of the class. Styles knew that during the week before break students were busy with finals and packing and getting their travel arrangements taken care of so he made a habit of keeping his classes short before break. For an elective critical thinking class, a heavy workload would only stress out his students which would undermine his goal of teaching them to think. He had been there.

Styles had been all over the world. His life views no longer aligned with his country of origin. Most had shifted to those of a global citizen. Styles was on a search for the thread that tied humanity together. His road was bumpy physically and metaphorically.

The God question came to him while living in between a Buddhist Temple and Muslim Mosque in SE Asia for two years where Styles had taught English to the children of the billionaire class. Each moring, almost in a competition for followers, Buddhist chantings would compete with the Muslim call to prayer. Both were piped through loudspeakers at full blast. Styles had gotten into the habit of setting his alarm before either would start so that he could wake up naturally instead of being forced awake by foreign sounds.

So it wasn't that he was against praying or God. Styles had faith. He just did not believe God should be sold like capitalism. Brands competing for devout consumers to buy their products. Spiritual Enlightenment versus Enlightened Spirituality is how he defined it when asked much like the Denver Broncos versus the NY Giants, Android versus IOS, Coke versus Pepsi and the heated debates that many had over diets. To Styles, he saw different religions as just different forms of transportation going to the same destination. Even ardent atheists he believed were grouped into the faithful in a loose fashion. They were all headed to death. Different faiths, atheists included, were all answering the same question: What happens after death? Some just seemed to create a carrot answer that was used to control and dictate how many lived in the now.

CHAPTER 26

When school resumed after winter break, so did the Triune's meetings in the second floor study room of the library overlooking the quad. Each had returned with a different story and their first order of business was to share.

Sally had been sent to Hawaii for a running camp. In the last match of the cross country season she had placed first and had moved up in the national rankings. She was now being groomed not only to walk at the Olympics but to actually run.

In the flash of a pan she had moved from an amateur athlete to a professional one. She had picked up a few sponsors including one who paid for her training camp including the transportation costs. She had arrived to find summer and had spent the four week holiday eating, sleeping, running and recovering on repeat. Sometimes late in the night she would find time to fire off some texts to her friends but most nights fell asleep on her way to the pillow.

She arrived back in NJ tanned and eager to connect back with Rachel and Charlie. Truth was, she never tired of running, but did tire of it being the only topic discussed. Many of her fellow athletes had a one track mind. She did not. Her mind wanted more to life and that is why she loved her time in the second floor study room of the library overlooking the quad.

Rachel had planned to drive back West when she was met by a surprise at the door. It rang. She opened the door to see her parents, Doug and Judy, standing at the threshold, coffee in hand and a taxi pulling away from the curb.

Then the night before made sense. Charlie and Sally had been adamant about cleaning up before they left under the excuse that Rachel shouldn't have to come home to a dirty home after break. She smiled and welcomed her parents into her home gladly accepting the offering of coffee.

"So you see, we never went on a honeymoon and we have never been to NY so we decided what the heck?" explained Doug. "We will spend a few nights in NY, see a show or two, eat some different foods before driving with you back home. We figured you'd welcome the company."

Rachel beamed. "Great."

"And thank Charlie and Sally," Judy stated. "They were in on it too. We had all exchanged numbers over Thanksgiving, but it was Mr. Romantic here," Judy poked Doug's ribs, "who came up with the idea. Just 15 years too late. But they did help to make sure you would be here to greet us and here you are."

Rachel now understood why she had had the feeling that Charlie and Sally were hiding something from them. Her mind had raced to find a solution and the only one she could find was that they had fallen in love and wanted to be a couple. Now she knew that was not to be the case.

Charlie had been offered a job as a snowboarding instructor at the local mountain. It paid well and he had spent the break saving money for his summer trip which he was planning. A backpack from the border of Mexico down to Panama. His parents and he had a trip planned for spring break to France to visit Geraldyne's mom and Charlie's grandma who was getting older by the day, probably to say goodbye.

"So now that we are all caught up, what about that God question before break? Make any headway?" Sally asked eager to start discussing something other than running.

They dove in head first and at midnight had agreed about their findings. They agreed that it seemed a waste of time to argue whether or not God existed. It was personal and most likely, similar to someone's sexuality. You either believed or didn't but trying to convince someone otherwise seemed fruitless.

Which brought them to a discussion about 'what is God?'. This took most of the night. They all had to come to terms with the vastness and infiniteness of space and time. As Anzaldua would suggest, the conception of God was a border. It was simultaneously the biggest of big, the smallest of small and all in the middle.

Where man seemed to err was in defining God in human terms with limited language. They discussed Shakespeare and how he had been limited by language writing about the common man and had to invent 10,000 plus words just to write his plays and make his points. It would only make sense, if an actual man was known to have this problem writing and defining his ideas, that we would collectively have the same problem writing about and defining God.

So that seemed to be the conundrum. They could all see that language was the limiting factor in defining and discussing God. The words needed to do it simply didn't and would not ever exist no matter how many more thousands of words were added. 'How does one define the undefinable?' and the subsequent answer was simple. We can't. We can only do our best at sharing how 'We', the singular not the plural, define and see God.

Then we either accept God as is or we argue and debate an undebatable unarguable topic. A fool's errand is like arguing that the Earth is flat or that the Sun revolves around the Earth. The

Sun is a static ball of fire in the sky. It is and will be there until it goes out and we cease to exist. The Earth is a sphere that revolves around the sun. This has been proven and the proof is in the technology we use daily like the internet and GPS. It's based on a round Earth.

Humans may want to argue these points but the argument has no direct impact on the facts. The Sun is a star of one of billions in the night sky. And every so often, like Shakespeare and his words, someone redefines our understanding of how ALL of it works. These men and women transcend humanity and become creators for a moment with their contributions. Copernicus. Galileo. Franklin. Einstein. Still, none believed they were God.

The night ticked away and as dawn approached, the Triune ended with the idea that whether or not God exists doesn't matter. What matters is that humanity has some stop gaps. That humanity doesn't become rabid, attacking and killing whimsically which sadly the direction they saw humanity headed. That the communal God that 'We' agree on in limited numbers, religions, are those stops that keep most of us from becoming nothing more than violent animals or beasts.

They imagined and discussed back in the day of creating 'The Language Limited God Edition'. That it was done so as a means of control, not for personal salvation or out of some sense of an intrinsic need for spirituality or the betterment of man. That, they believed, would come later.

First and foremost, God was created as a boogeyman to give value and create fear of those at the top of the humanities' pyramid. Pre-God, man was more animalistic by nature. Fending for itself and its offspring. Once communication and language were created, then came the hierarchical system which put a few at the top and the rest of us at the bottom. And every so often, some at the bottom rise up against the top and those at the top would be replaced. It was a cycle much like how we see the lion kingdom playout.

It was only after the top lion created a myth that supported their control did the power pyramid become more static and rigid with less challenges to the throne. Myths like, 'I will protect you from the monsters in the forest. All you have to do is provide me with a carrot, a rabbit and a jug of water.' From then on, it was just fine-tuning the myths of the monster to meet the needs and changing knowledge of man.

When we found out that lightning was caused by storms and not Zeus, we rebranded Zeus and his family of many gods as the monotheistic God we know today. And as knowledge grew, so did the story of God until we arrived at the modern day version. The one in which few created a narrative, with their limited language, for the rest of us. Then, we were forced to believe the myths for fear of death at the hands of those at the top for crimes like blasphemy and witchery. Our freedom to define something undefinable was taken from us and in its place was put someone else's definition that we were forced to accept for fear of death in the present and hell in the future.

Today, God is the path to heaven. That is what they hawk and sell. God as a product. Not God as our own personal undefinable indescribable connection with life, love, the world and All things we hold dear. Instead, we are taught by religious sellers with fancy names like priest, pastor, rabi, pujari, bhikkhu and imams worldwide that their definitions are the true path and ours are false or misguided. That we are incapable of living correctly. That we need their products and them to teach us how to live in the present to prepare for the future and one way is to temper man's desire to be the lion and rise up against those the sellers protect.

By the time the Triune were finished, they were done thinking, wired and ready to go.

"I think that about sums up where we are at with the God

question," Rachel stated. "Anyone interested in heading back to my place and making it messy again?"

"You read my mind," said Sally with Charlie agreeing with a smile and a nod.

They collected their belongings and headed back to Rachel's home where they made love until the first light of morning when they fell asleep together for a few hours before heading back to the reality of school and their classes.

CHAPTER 27

Whenever Charlie woke up in a tangle of limbs, he was grateful. Rachel was more dominant and Sally more submissive in bed. One liked to be taken and the other took with Charlie somewhere in the middle.

He awoke and climbed out of bed heading to the bathroom then to the kitchen to make coffee. Bringing two women coffee in bed was one of the highlights of his short life thus far.

"Good morning. Coffee here."

"Mmm. Smells good and thanks for letting me sleep in," Sally answered. "I love sleeping in. Waking up to run is a grind some days. I always look forward to rest days but am always so grateful to be running when I go early. A catch 22, but a good one."

"Morning babes," Rachel beamed. "Sorry if I was a bit rough last night Charlie."

"All is good. I'll tell you when you are." He winked.

Sexually they were exploring each other in any way they could imagine and all were being satisfied in ways they had not yet tried before.

"So what do you think Styles has in store for us today?"

"Don't know," answered Charlie.

They finished their coffee. Took turns taking showers with Sally opting to make breakfast while Rachel made the bed and cleaned up.

When they were ready to go, they grabbed their bags and books and headed out the door. Arriving at the lecture hall, they found Styles sitting like he did waiting for class to begin.

Styles had learned on the first day of his first year of teaching that having the reputation of getting to class before the students paid off in spades. The early kids got a few more minutes with their teacher, the on-time kids felt respected for no time wasted and the late kids either changed their ways or their class. They were ostracized by their peers, not their teacher.

Pleasantries were given to teacher and students alike and when the bell rang, all got ready to work.

"As some of you may have seen, this past weekend there was some big news that will have an effect on my teaching and your learning. Any guesses?" Styles pointed to a boy a few rows back who rarely raised his hand.

"Are you talking about the Presidential debate between Willy Green and Jan Slogan?" he asked.

"Yes. At face value this is a debate between a conservative and a liberal. A marine and a hippie. But in reality it is so much more. Since watching it unfold on social media, in the news and across late night TV, I thought today we could shift gears to the topic at hand.

"As you know, I rarely just speak or lecture but in this instance I think it behooves us that I do so to lay the groundwork for the ensuing debate. Plus, this is my class so I am the boss."

Styles laughed at himself and the class followed suit.

"I went backwards to go forward over the weekend. I started

to examine when the line between fact and fiction became so blurred. I, also, chose not to go back so far that this would become a rant against organized religion and global and historical leadership and politics. That seemed too easy. So I chose to start at an easier point to access and fine-tuned the question I wanted to ponder.

"I came up with this. When did modern society begin to accept fiction as fact? The answer that I came up with was WWE wrestling. Prior to WWE, we understood where we needed to put on our 'suspension of the disbelief' hats and glasses. We knew when we were watching fact or fiction and certainly knew when we were reading it. The labels to differentiate the two needed to be clear. Libraries and bookstores, where most bought or borrowed books pre-Amazon, were and still are clearly labeled. Fact or story. So a video of the Olympics would be classified and labeled and put with other non-fiction videos. On the other hand, a video depicting the highlights of WWF Wrestlemania 23, for example, would be classified and shelved in the entertainment section along with other sports films like Chariots of Fire and Rocky. WWE is a story. It is a modern day adult sport based soap opera. Nothing more. Nothing less. The actors just happen to also be athletes who work hard at making the fights look real to their audience and do a good job of it.

"How many of you have found yourselves sucked into an hour or two of WWE wrestling while channel surfing or YouTubing?" Styles asked with almost all hands going up.

"But what is interesting is that many fans now, and some may be in this room, believe that WWE is a sport. It is not. It is a modern day soap opera, and the producers want it to be seen as such. They want fans to believe in the hero-villain narrative that is being sold and to take sides. The problem is that so many believe the narrative to be true and argue their opinion with fervor. And this brings me to the next level of devolution of sport and entertainment is MMA.

"MMA is modern day sports entertainment. It blurs the lines between sport and story and does so perfectly for the non-thinker. Remember, we can go to Greece and Italy and Turkey to see its origins and where sport evolved from. MMA is nothing more than gladiating and gladiating is nothing more than a cock or dog fight between two violent animals. It is not a sport. It is a fight to the death as entertainment with the hopes that a referee stops the fight before a fighter dies. It's a street fight. It's a war. It is entertainment to the mad but it is not a sport. A sport has sportsmanship. We enjoy MMA because it satisfies our blood lust. Our desire to see others in harm's way as long as it's not us. A car accident is a perfect example. Almost all of us look.

"This being said, over the course of the last fifty or so years, the line between fact and fiction and sport and entertainment has been blurred to the point that our 'suspension of the disbelief' glasses no longer work properly. And as sport has devolved to needing PEDs to compete and soap opera storylines to garner viewership so has news; how we get it and how we perceive it.

"The News is no longer just the facts delivered to the viewer in the most non-bias way possible. Instead, the news is a product that needs viewership or subscriptions to survive. The news, when developed for primetime, was viewed as a modern day necessity. It was funded by the state and needed to be non-bias and present the facts and the truth or it lost funding and was canceled. Today, it is not. We tune in, not to the broadcaster whose voice we like the best, but the channel that we know is supporting our political points of view. Conservative news. Christian news. Atheist news. Liberal news. No longer is news written to the center. It is now written to connect with a side. That is no longer news. It is infotainment and should be labeled as such.

"We should stop allowing lies and misinformation to be sold as truth. We should label infotainment as clearly as we do cigarettes because the damage is just as bad. What society is giving up is its ability and freedom to think rationally and come to decisions based on the whole picture. Instead, we are allowing ourselves to blindly follow products and sources that are clearly echo chambers and information silos designed with only one purpose. Make money for the owner by filling seats or selling ads. We are creating a world owned by Facebook and the like, and movies like Idiocracy and Don't Look Up are becoming biopics about the devolution of man's reason and ability to think rationally. Instead of comedic interludes about unfortunate mistakes we may make in the future, these films are capturing clearly the mistakes we are making presently.

"If you don't start to look around for the truth, you will find yourself living a life that is based on someone else's opinion and probably lies. Lies are easier to handle than truths especially when the truth may hurt or uncover something ugly about yourself or society. So I challenge you to examine who you are today and how you have arrived here in the now to see if you can find some threads to pull that may reveal in part, places where you have bought into fiction instead of fact.

CHAPTER 28

While many students arrived at college knowing who they were and how to learn, a few would continue to struggle with their identity and between a fixed and a growth mindset. Styles was of the mind that college was a luxury, not a right and that the system was broken and needed fixing. Trade schools should still scatter the educational landscape with the primary purpose of providing and placing students into needed professions.

Some, no matter how hard you pushed them to, could not think for themselves. They could only succeed in classes and professions in which the hierarchy was clear and the tasks laid out. The military was like this. It followed a clear chain of command and success was derived from a cadets ability to successfully complete orders. Restaurants too. The theater. Lots of industries, he knew, were run like this. It was that some were either wired biologically or by circumstance to need the safety net of succeeding by doing, not thinking.

AU was a thinkers school trying to meld the borders between rigid and open thinking by fostering the creative minds of its students. Some succeeded after AU beyond measure. Their alumni list was growing globally with people of note. But some still failed. Donald looked to be on that course.

"That is class is so stupid. This guy is trying to tear down politics and religion. Who does he think he is?" Donald asked Terry as they left class and walked across the quad.

"I hear ya Donny but I think Styles is just trying to get a reaction," Terry responded. "Me, I know that this is just a stopping point. In a few years I'll be back home working for the family company. My life is pretty planned out. This is the only time I'll get to really try to think outside the box."

"That's all good and well, but me, I want success. You know that and Styles seems to be getting in my way. He's challenging the system that got me here. The system works. That's why our country is the best in the world. It's not because we think, it's because we do. We build. Styles wants to get rid of that," said Donald.

Terry knew where he fit. He was plain. He lived very comfortably within the box. He didn't ask for much yet he had enough wealth to not want for much. He was a normal nice person. Not boring but not confrontational. He rolled with life. Always had. He didn't spend much time questioning things and was not a standout in anything. He was middle of the road. Not a blank canvas but more like a framed picture in a hotel that is never noticed. He had other friends at school, but he liked Donald because Donald was the first person to ever treat him as an equal as opposed to a wallflower or side dish.

But this is where they disagreed and those disagreements seemed to be coming in shorter and shorter intervals. Terry liked Styles. He liked hearing what Styles had to say and watching and listening to others respond. Somewhere in his mind threads were being pulled and he could sometimes see light past the gray or fog as to what they were uncovering.. He had never been expected to think on his own so being asked to at college and by Styles was foreign. It was something that was taking some time to get used to.

"I think you have to give Styles a break. He's just trying to get us to think man. Yeah, some of the stuff he suggests is too weird for me but some of it is interesting. Think about the deconstruction of God as a monster in the forest. I can imagine that. Some mother trying to convince her son not to go into the woods. She tries everything and finally says, 'Oh, did I not mention the monsters that eat little boys in the forest?' and then boys finally listen. I am sure things like this have happened throughout history. It only makes sense. It doesn't change faith or God. It doesn't undermine anything. It just gets us to see things a little more clearly. It's like X-Men and Wolverine. He existed within the group and without, and because of that, he was the most interesting character. Anzaldua would have liked him. He was a borderland character. And the last few films were his origin story and that's a trend. We are no longer as fascinated with the epic and the big battles as we are with the origin of how things have come to be. And I think that is what Styles is getting us to think about. Not Jesus as the son of God but Jesus as a troubled teen or Moses or Abraham and Mohammad or Siddartha or whomever. If any of them had transitioned from boy to man, they found their penises. What did they do with them? He's trying to get us to think. That's it. To think about things in a different way so that we have a clear picture of history so that we can choose more wisely. I know my choices because I kind of know my future. I will meet a woman someday, maybe here or back home, we will get married and have kids. On Sundays we will go to church. Saturdays will be family day. The week I will spend working at or running the family business until one of my kids takes over. This class isn't going to change that, but it may change how I think and interact with others. When I got here, I was of the mind that gays were bad because I am from a closed society that has taught me so. I can see that as not being 100% accurate. I would still probably not hire a gay but would not fire one just because. And those two girls, Rachel and Sally, I have a few classes with them, have certainly proven to me that girls can be equal to men. Would I date them? No. They would chew me up and spit me out. I want a subservient partner. I want a plain, normal life so I will wash this class off of me when I get back home, but for now, I will explore it. It's fun. It's why I don't understand your position on the class. It seems like you are just against it. Not that you don't get it, but that you don't want to get it. Doesn't matter to me either way. It's one class of many and this is just four years of a greater plan for me, but I'd suggest giving it a chance and giving Styles a break. ` `

"Whatever man," Donald answered. He was not yet ready for criticism or self exploration.

Their relationship was never the same. Terry, who had started out thinking he was beneath Donald as a student and young man, realized he was not. They still worked together for the class but it was apparent to Terry that he would have to do most of the work if he wanted to learn or uncover anything. Terry now saw that higher education was not about being smart but being able to think and he was trying to do just that.

"Professor Styles, do you have a minute?" Terry asked while knocking on Style's open office door.

"Sure. Take a seat and what can I do for you?"

"Something has changed since starting your class. I am not thinking the same. I am starting to see the world differently like I am exploring it through, please don't make fun, the 'origin story' lens like Wolverine or Superman."

"That sounds promising. Care to explain a bit more?" Styles asked.

"Are you familiar with 'origin stories'?" asked Terry.

"I am old but I do not live in a shoe. Yes, of course. I like some of them but think they do not dig enough with maybe the exception of Batman which at least gives it a good go."

"Good. Great. Yeah. That's what I mean. Since taking your class I am starting to explore the origins of things, not just the facts.

The stories. Like Newton sitting under the tree and discovering gravity. I am more interested in why he was sitting under the tree in the first place. Does that make . . ."

Styles erupted in laughter. "Does that make sense? Of course. That my child is learning. Congratulations you are a student now of the first order. You are a thinking man."

Terry was unsure how to respond. "Are you making fun of me?"

"Fun of you, Terry. No. You may in fact have just made my day. I always have students that are interested in the class and others who fight against it, but rarely do I have a student shift from one group to the other. And you have just done so in the most magnificent way possible through your own mind, your own interests by creating a story about something you have learned and other stories you are interested in. 'Origin story.' It's a perfect metaphor and lens to look through. I would recommend you to keep looking."

Terry left Syle's office a little less sure of his plain normal future and life. He had never received an accolade like that before but he was sure that he wanted to receive one like that again. To be commended for how he thought. It gave him hope and a new bounce in his stride as he left the office and walked across campus past the library with the light on in the second story study room overlooking the quad.

CHAPTER 29

Sally had been a success story in high school due to her natural running ability and work ethic but also the unfaltering support of her parents and coach. The first year of college had been easy. All she was expected to do was to show up to practice, do her best and demonstrate her ability to learn and improve. Easy. She had succeeded.

During Sally's second year, she placed in the top ten regularly and her coaches were still pleased. This was starting to change. She could see it in their eyes and in the attitude towards her in the locker room.

"Good job today girls," said team captain Beatrice. "Almost all of you had your fastest race kilometer ever. Good work."

Beatrice glared at Sally and the coldness could be felt between them. Beatrice was a natural collegiate level athlete. She knew her days were numbered as an athlete and her chances of winning another race were diminishing by the day. A senior, she was in the twilight of her running career.

"What gives?" Beatrice asked.

"I don't know what you mean," responded Sally.

"You have all this," Beatrice pointed at Sally, starting at her feet and stopping at her head. "You are the most gifted runner I have ever met and one of the most gifted runners the school has ever seen. But here you are. No improvement in 3 months. Again, what gives?"

Sally loved running and competition, but she hated this part of the sport. The Ego Blame. She had read about it, been warned about it and seen it in action, but had not experienced it until now. The problem with the Ego Blame was that part of it was true.

The Ego Blame is simple. It's when others blame the star for not being bright enough. Whether on purpose or not, the Ego Blame has doused many a star putting out their fire which once darkened is almost impossible to re-ignite.

Sally knew this. A quarterback being blamed for the championship loss never to be seen again. The Olympic hopeful whose name is splattered across the headlines only to never be heard of again during the games or after.

After the match Sally met the Triune in the small room in the top right corner of the second story of the library overlooking the quad. She was the last to arrive and quietly entered the room with eyes on her. She was not the beaming pony-tailed beauty they were used to seeing.

"What gives?" asked Rachel.

Sally laughed. "You know you are the second person to ask me that question today. Deja vu."

"Well," responded Charlie.

"I work really hard. You both know that. I wake-up early. Never miss a workout. I eat well. Sleep well. What? We have sex once a week. We don't drink or do drugs and I am at a plateau that I can't seem to get off of no matter how hard I try. Worst yet is that my teammates, coach and I expect more than I am able to deliver."

Most friends would react as a net. Rachel and Charlie were not nets. They knew that running was one of the career choices open to Sally. It wasn't a flash in the pan. A hobby to shelve after college or to be relived as the glory days of the past. It could be her job.

"Can you offer a little more detail? The brass tacks," asked Rachel.

"Yes. When I was six, I was a champion on my first go and I progressed as time went by. I got stronger, faster and luckily, taller. I have a body that's designed to be a good mid-distance runner. In junior year of high school I went under 4:40 for the mile and came in second at nationals. I was a small town celebrity and with that came coaches knocking on the door.

"I spoke to Oregon and Texas and Colorado and none fit the mold that I was looking for. You know this. I want to be an athlete until I retire. Then, I want to do something else with my intellect. So I was careful and chose AU. The school has a great reputation, a state of the art track and regularly comes in the top 5 at collegiate nationals. When I met the coach, I was all in. Coach Jones is second to none. She knows her game and knows how to keep her players focused and improving.

"But she has a huge team to manage. In high school, I was the star. I knew it. The coach knew it. The team knew it. And it was easy. Here, I have the opportunity to be a star at the national level, but I am not getting there. I can regularly run a sub 4:35 in competition but that doesn't even get me into the top 5. I am not improving. I need to make a jump and I think I need help."

"Well, help is here. What can we offer? We got your back," Charlie said and Rachel agreed.

The next night Sally arrived a few minutes after the others. She was agasp when she entered the small little room in the top right corner of the second story of the library overlooking the quad. Sitting in the usual empty chair was Coach Jones.

Over the next hour, Charlie and Rachel became quick studies on running and how best to support their friend.

"I think there are a few things you could do to help Sally to shave three seconds," Coach Jones stated.

"Shoot. We are all ears," said Charlie.

"One for all, all for one," Rachel snorted finishing off with, "ugh, so cheesy. Vomit."

They all laughed.

"Okay. To help Sally, number one, wake up with her especially on her days with slow morning workouts and go with her. You will be dying but she will be tempered and forced to stay slow. On her fast mornings, bike alongside of her and make sure she is going fast enough. I'll send you the data. Beyond that, if she is not in class or studying, she should be legs up in bed resting. Help her with her chores and get her off of her feet. That's it."

Rachel looked at Charlie. Charlie looked back at Rachel and then looked at Sally. Sally shrugged in agreement. Charlie and Rachel shrugged back and then shrugged to Coach Jones, okay. And that was that. For the rest of spring, Sally's 3 seconds became the focus of the Triune. They cooked and cleaned and woke up early to help support their friend the best way they could.

Mid-April at regionals Sally ran a 4:28:40 breaking 4:30 for the first time in her career and podiuming for the first time at AU with a bronze third place.

Back in the locker room Beatrice gave a loud cheer of support for the team with a special shout out to Sally.

"I knew it. I knew you could do it," proclaimed Beatrice.

"Thanks Bea," replied Sally.

For the rest of the season and beyond, Beatrice and Sally

became close friends with Beatrice monitoring the successes and failures of Sally from afar and calling on occasion to offer congratulations or a kick in the butt when needed.

CHAPTER 30

When the alarm buzzed and the Triune awoke, two things were abundantly clear. One, it was early. Two, Rachel and Charlie were not practiced at waking up this early and neither completely understood the fitness level of their compatriot. The plan was for Rachel to make breakfast and Charlie to ride his bike with Sally. Each got ready for work.

"What's the plan this morning?" Charlie asked.

"Easy 5km. 6:15 pace."

"Cool. I will run." Charlie said and leaned the bike up against the wall in the hall of the apartment. "Easy. Right?"

Sally responded, "Yes. Easy."

They started with a few static stretches and were off.

Charlie was one of the many who thought being an athlete was relatively easy taking dedication and practice. In middle and high school he would bike, run, climb or play frisbee with friends while barely catching a sweat. At AU, he played ultimate frisbee in the quad once a week. It got his heart pumping; he never thought it was something to write home about.

They started to jog. Sally was quite talkative. Charlie was not.

"I can't tell you how much I appreciate this. You and Rachel are the best. Thanks so much."

"No problem," Charlie responded through gritted teeth.

"I never thought to ask you two but the support is awesome. Watch out up here. The next km is a false flat."

"No worries," Charlie said while thinking in between gasps what the 'F' is a false flat.

It turned out to be a hill. To call it a false flat was a lie. He was in pain for those six minutes. Barely able to breath, legs burning and body screaming to stop while Sally and her pony tail bobbed and swayed ahead of him turning every 20 seconds or so with a beaming face and a grand smile saying things like 'you're doing great' and 'not much farther.' When she said another 30 seconds and we will head back, Charlie nodded through open eyes and a fake smile.

"How was it?" asked Rachel, handing both a recovery drink in a bottle while they stretched outside.

"Easy and thank you so much, Rachel," responded Sally as she took a sip.

"What about you Charlie?"

"Three words. Easy my ass. Rachel, I recommend riding the bike with her, not running."

They all laughed and for the next few days, Charlie was on breakfast and clean-up duty while the girls headed out and they both laughed regularly at him as he hobbled around campus the next few days aching like he had never ached before. After the male ego bruising, Charlie's perspective about athleticism took an immediate 180.

Charlie over breakfast one morning said,"I don't think I ever gave your running a lot of thought. I am a fan but I would never have guessed how much work it actually takes to be you. Awesome. And to think on race day, you run twice as fast as me bleeding out of my eyes and wanting to vomit on your easy day. I just didn't really understand the difference. Wow. Champion."

"I think he has finally started to understand the pecking order," replied Rachel towards Sally.

"Yeah. I think he has," Sally replied to Rachel and then to all she said, "lesson learned."

"On my next rest day over a weekend, we can all go to the park and trail run. Before I met you two, I went there at least once a week. And you would be surprised how most men either tried to race me or pick me up. Charlie, I have bruised a lot of male egoes."

One of the reasons why Sally had chosen AU was its proximity to nature and trails to run on. In the first few months she would go quite regularly and many times she had to ward off men who thought they were all that.

If the mood hit, she would have fun with it. Once, there had been a man who had tried really hard to get her attention but had never been ready to run at the same time. He was either finishing his run when Sally arrived or vice versa, or he was still getting ready when Sally bounced out of her car and headed up the trail. Once, the stars had aligned.

"I've seen you here often but I have never seen you on the trail. Do you usually only do the short or long loop?" the runner asked, eyeing Sally.

"Do you usually do the long loop? What is that like 15km?"

"Fifteen kms of technical running. It's a beast. By the way, Ted here."

"I'm Sally. I am at AU. 15km. Huh?"

"You want to try it with me and I'll buy you a coffee after."

"Sure. Sounds good. Lead the way."

They headed through the gate and onto the trail. Ted was chatting and talking about how accomplished of a runner he was and that he managed a small restaurant in town serving fusion food. Portobello hamburgers and tofu caesar salads.

"How's the pace?" Ted asked. "Holding on okay. Still 13.5 to go," while glancing down at his watch.

"It's fine. If you want, you can step up the pace a bit. I'd like to see if I can hold on."

Ted took the bait. His ego had been challenged. He ratcheted up the pace to his threshold. Sally knew this because he kept looking at his watch to see some sort of reading and data.

That was until he faltered, running over an off-camber section. Not falling but slowing down just enough to force Sally into the lead. She passed him and kept going. She never saw Ted again. She guessed he started running at either a different trail or at a different time.

It was amazing to her how many people made everything into a competition even in things in which they had limited or little experience. They always seemed to have the best gear from head to toe and an air of superiority. Men and women alike. It was a personality type. And they never looked like they were having fun. Like running was a chore. That was until Sally would jog by them like they were standing still. They would huff and puff and try to keep up. Sally assumed that they imagined few were faster than them. This happened with the 'Beast' type often. Instead of learning and following, they were always in race mode which in fact made them slow.

"Thanks Charlie. I probably should have told you to ride the bike but I couldn't help it."

"No worries. I'll get you back someday when I can walk normally again."

"Was it really that hard?" asked Rachel.

"No. I'm probably just out of shape. You should give it a go too," Charlie said to Rachel while winking at Sally.

"I think I might just do that."

Two days later, Rachel was hobbling around the kitchen making breakfast while Charlie raised the seat on the bicycle to pedal alongside Sally. Now, Rachel knew too.

CHAPTER 31

Rachel was often described as crazy and dismissed by others. For those who got to know her, she was abrupt and brilliant. She could deconstruct a system finding its truths and flaws in a New York minute and when it came to AU, she was known by the dean by both her fans and not.

"Can you believe the gaul of this girl?" asked Professor Glory Westford. "In this work, which she wants to send off to be peer reviewed and published, she attacks the pillars of Anzaldua and this institution. She should be expelled immediately."

"Let's not jump to any conclusions. Let's hear Rachel's side of the story first," Dean Aysegul Yoltas responded.

"So you are just going to allow her to paint the school the fool. Maybe I should go to the board. See about your job. There are others who would support my decision."

"I cannot and will not tell you what to do. That is your choice. I will also not be threatened. I understand that this student has hit a nerve. It happens. Don't let your frustration get the best of you, Glory. That is my advice because I can see that it is."

"You are a fool, Dean. Let's get this over with."

The two were sitting in Dean's office. Yoltas sat behind her desk with a window, similar to the one in the library, overlooking the quad. Westford was sitting in one of two chairs in front of the desk that Yoltas had made sure were level with her own. She did not like looking down on others or the power she felt when she did. On the other side of the door sat Rachel.

Dean Yoltas lifted the receiver on her phone, pressed a button and asked her secretary to send Rachel in.

"They are ready for you dear. You may go in."

Rachel had written an essay in which she explored the idea that almost all people wore multiple hats and lived in some sort of metaphorical borderland. Then went on to state that those who weren't, were pretty much rigid, racist, misogynist, religious or just plain dumb. They crammed and stuffed themselves into boxes that stopped them from thinking like a corset of the mind or a shoe too small for the foot. It fit only with pain or discomfort and forced the wearer to get used to the pain.

Westford was a full professor on the tenure track who some students respected, none admired and a few couldn't stand. Rachel was in the last group. She found Westford to be small minded and unable to think despite having a PhD next to her name.

Westford had earned a commuter PhD. She had spent 15 years going to night school once a week and had received a PhD in return. No one believed her to be brilliant or worthy of the title with the exception of herself. She was not well traveled or well read. She had succeeded thus far by showing up and playing the game well.

On the first day of class she introduced herself as Dr. Westford and wanted to be called as such by her students. Stating that she would not respond to any other name. Few understood how she had fallen into the position and less liked her air of superiority.

"Come in Rachel. Please sit down." Yoltas said, pointing to the chair next to Westford. "We have a few questions for you."

"Go ahead," Rachel responded after taking a seat.

"Do you know why you are here?" asked Ingram.

"Yes," Rachel said looking out the window onto the quad but being perceived as looking at the dean.

"Dr. Westford has some concerns about an essay that you have written that she believes undermines the very foundation and pillars of this school and that you want to publish the work."

"It's my work. I don't see the problem and yes, I want to publish it. But no, my work does not go against the foundation of the school."

"How can you say that?" queried Westford. "You suggest that almost all people live on a metaphorical borderland. That is simply not true. If it had been, Anzaldua would have written it into her theory, don't you think? And furthermore her theory would have no weight. She was looking at what makes one group different. Not what connects all."

Nothing made Rachel more livid than guided questions used to elicit a response. Nothing. She had always been okay with differences of opinion, agreement or disagreement and uncovering new ideas. She couldn't stand being forced to take a side no matter the topic.

"Westford is accusing you of deliberately writing a piece of work that will cast shade on this institution and the legacy of Anzaldua. That is why you are here. I would recommend stating your case," said Dean Yoltas.

"My case. My case? Am I on trial? I guess I am. Okay. Then, Dean Yoltas, I have one question for you. Did you read the work in question?"

"No, I have not."

"I don't see what this has to do with you making a mockery of the school," exclaimed Westford.

"It's fine Dr. Westford. Please, Rachel, continue."

Rachel went on to explain what she had written and the process by which she arrived there. The basic premise of the Borderlands is duplicity; the ability to shapeshift from one form to another and back again. But you know this. What I suggested is that the concept of Neplanta is present in all people. Like gravity. It's there and I think most people put on different hats without ever really questioning it or identifying it. They just live. Gravity does its thing. They do theirs. Those that don't are the problem. Rachel glanced at Westford.

And then one day, one morning running with Sally, it popped into my mind how many times my education was splattered with the term 'lifelong learner' and what it meant. It was a moment of clarity. The best teachers out there talk and emulate what it means to be a lifelong learner. In many ways, lifelong learners live on the borderland between student and teacher and seamlessly move back and forth between both roles. They are simultaneously students and teachers learning and teaching. Most teachers arrive here by gravity. They are teachers at heart. They have a calling and are gifted with the skill of being a teacher but also understand that sometimes they are also the student. This is a lifelong learner. Both, together.

Coaches are a great example of this. Most, no longer, are at the same play level as their athletes or mentees, but have the ability to help those they coach move past them. They guide their athletes to teacher level or mastery and when this occurs, coaches return back to being students. They have to. The shining stars reinvent the game. The rules of play change.

Only a losing coach or teacher thinks otherwise. The ones that believe they are right and therefore the student is wrong based on some historical or antiquated thinking. This suggests that mastery is unattainable. That the border is impossible to cross.

It is not. It is not easy but it is not unsurmountable. Yet, there are many teachers who teach only. They think in their box and push their wares without allowing the student to assume the role of the teacher. These teachers are rigid in their thinking and rigidity is not a strength.

A lifelong learner is a fancy way of saying student and those who have a desire to stop being a student, live in a small rigid box. All lifelong learners move past them or just use them as a stepping stone to grow. They offer nothing. Only an example of what not to be.

"That is what I wrote about. It celebrates and defines the pillars and foundation of AU; it does not undermine it as some might think."

"Can you believe this?" asked Westford. "To think, a student condemning teachers for knowing the answers and expecting students to learn them. It's foolish immature thinking."

Dean Yoltas had heard enough. She has long suspected that Westford had been a poor hire. Someone who had cleverly crafted a resume and was professionally prepared for the interview.

At her core, Yoltas knew who Westford was. She was simply an organizer with an amiable personality that most peers didn't find offensive. As a dean, Yoltas excelled because most simply liked her and respected her work. There was a world of difference.

Before being a dean, Yoltas had been a high school math teacher. She had a Bachelor's in Higher Math and a Masters in Education, and had been hired out of college to be a teacher. On day one she knew that she was not a master teacher but loved being around students and at the school. She went back to school at night and earned her PhD in Administrative Education.

Her philosophy was simple. Teachers were teachers and she

would support them as such. She would get out of there way. She was a manager. That was her skill. To run the school, not to teach the students. She expected that her teachers were professionals and able to do their jobs with limited, if any, interference. The successful and respected teachers she rarely interacted with. The failing ones found reason to sit in the chair across from her regularly. Westford was one who kept the seat warm coming across as a teacher who believed students were out to get her.

"I see. I think I understand now. Rachel, can you please sit outside again for a minute?"

Rachel agreed and left.

"Dr. Westford," Yoltas pondered before speaking. "When I walked into the classroom for the first time many years ago, I saw that I was not fit for a career as a teacher so, like you, I went back to school, earned a PhD and here I have sat for 15 years helping to support and diffuse problems as they arise."

"Are you siding with her?" asked Westford. "She is wet behind the ears. She wants to suggest that students know more than teachers. That is against the fabric of education, and the fact that she is unable to see her mistake and take criticism for her ideas, demonstrates her weakness as a student."

"Maybe. I need some time to think about how to handle this situation. I will get back to you soon. Thank you for your time, Dr. Westford." Yoltas rose and showed Westford to the door, and beckoned Rachel back into the office.

Rachel came back in and sat again in the chair across from the desk staring out the window overlooking the quad. She liked looking out at the quad. It gave her peace. Trees. Students crossing back and forth. Birds flying. She found solace there.

"I will make this brief. I know you don't like to mince words. I don't either. My advice is this. I would not make an enemy out of Dr. Westford. I would sit on your work until the time is right.

Take that for what it is worth."

"Okay," Rachel stood up and left.

Dean Yoltas snickered and laughed the moment Rachel had left the office. She knew that this was not the end but the beginning. More than anything Yoltas wanted to take Rachel's side and filet Dr. Westford publicly for being a dimwit. Rachel was correct. Too many teachers believed that what they were selling was a product that needed to be packaged and bought as such. Ingram knew that master teachers did not think this way. They all agreed on one premise and that was that some of the best lessons they were ever taught were at the hands of their students.

CHAPTER 32

"Y
ou were right about Westford, Charlie. I should have heeded your warning."

During Charlie's freshman year he had had a run in with Dr. Westword that led to him receiving his only B thus far.

Westford's History 101 class started like his others and like many teachers, Westford started her classes with a lecture and students were expected to take notes.

On the day it had gone south for Charlie, Westford had started with a lecture about the feminism in history. It was the type of idea that bugged Charlie. He had been taught by bad example not to live in the world of would'ves, could'ves, and should'ves. They were dead ends. Unfortunately, Westford had written her thesis about a dead end subject that Charlie could see as light as day. A truck could drive through the primary hole or flaw in her argument.

It was why Styles' class about libraries had been so interesting. They had arrived among the thrall of students into class on which the board there was written one word: Library. They had all looked around and stared at each other asking the same question, are we headed to the library today?

The answer was no and Styles, a moment after the bell rang, told the students to take a seat and settle down. He did not believe in telling students to get ready. Students learned at their own pace and in their own way.

"Libraries are almost sacred places. We go to them for many reasons. To learn. To research. To think. To read. For some, to get warm. And what is beautiful about libraries is that they are ours. They are free to use in exchange for the taxes we pay.

"Libraries are also a place to learn about freedom, especially freedom of speech. A friend once said to me, 'my freedom begins where someone else's ends.' There is no other place where that line is so clear. Fiction to the left. Non-fiction to the right. Two Dewey decimal systems. One to organize facts with numbers and letters and one to organize stories with letters only. And libraries from north to south and east to west use this system to allow their patrons to easily decipher between truths and lies. Real and make believe.

Today, those lines are blurred. That is clear. Look at the headlines for a week and you will find that not a week will go by without a headline that puts truth and lies on trial either physically in a court or metaphorically in the minds of the public. Truth is at war with lies. Sometimes I think we should get all the librarians together and have them solve many of the world's problems since they are the guardians of fact and fiction. Not judges or lawyers or politicians, but librarians. Their purpose is to draw the line in the sand.

But as more and more people frequent Google and Twitter and FB for data, the job of the librarian gets pushed closer to the waste bin and once trashed, the guardians of the line between truth and lies will perish for a long time if not forever.

Problem is our reality is based on the line that is drawn. Who draws the line, owns the truth. We should be careful who we are giving the stick.

"But enough lecturing. Brass tacks time. Imagine you are a

librarian. By a show of hands, decide where these titles will be placed. Fiction to the left. Nonfiction to the right."

"Don Quixote."

All left hands shot up.

"A Biography of President Jimmy Carter."

All right hands shot up.

"The Complete Works of Shakespeare." Left hands up.

"A Brief History of the Globe Theater." Right hands only.

"So far so good. The Highlight Reel of the Last Super Bowl?"

A moment passed before right hands went up.

"The highlight reel of MMA."

A few lefts and a few rights.

"The Titanic starring Dicaprio?"

Same. Some left. Some right.

Before TV and Film, the lines were clear. The job of the librarian was made easy. Facts to the right. Stories to the left. But today, those lines are blurred. We are taught that sport is Fact yet many of you voted for MMA to be filed with stories when asked about it. Why is that? It's because the lines are blurred. I would argue that a lot of what we watch as real is more fiction than fact. Doping athletes rigging the game. The doping is a fact but by doping, the outcome of the game is not fair or truthful therefore probably not a fact based on library standards. The librarian's job in the modern day is more difficult and is made so by our disinterest in keeping that line clear. We are giving away the truth.

In that moment Charlie smiled realizing exactly why he had had such a hard time with Westford. She had wanted the class to view history through the lens of a matriarchy. Charlie could remember the request as if it were yesterday and he also could remember his response and those of the class behind him.

In his freshman year, briefly, Charlie had opted to sit in the front of the class. He wanted to have little distance between him and the teacher. Less distractions. Westford's class had taught him that physical distance was more useful for students like him. One's that would question teachers and sometimes needed a safe place to blend and hide.

Charlie raised his hand and Westford called on him.

"I don't agree with your premise that history should be looked at through the lens of feminism. It didn't exist until the late 19th century. Like gravity. Science wasn't using gravity as a lens to view science until it was discovered. Same thing with other facts and theories like the world being a globe and not flat. Until it was discovered, all thought differently. The discoveries themselves created the changes in our collective thinking. No one, male or female, was thinking regularly through a feminist lens until feminism was uncovered."

As Charlie spoke he could see Westford go flush but he had already started the ball rolling. He just didn't yet realize the ball was his head.

"I have a PhD in Women's Studies. You do not. You are here to learn. You are proving you cannot."

A voice in the back could be heard saying, 'I agree with the guy in the front' which was immediately followed with sounds of agreement from most of the class behind him. Charlie had accidentally led a mutiny in which his head was the one rolling down the grading scale. For the rest of Westford's class, Charlie had opted to change his seat and try his best to keep his mouth shut.

"Westford is the antithesis of Styles. He's trying to get us to think. She is trying to get her students to follow. She sucks. Sorry Rachel. If I had known, I would have warned you."

"She is a witch," Rachel responded.

"She wanted us to view the world through a lens that she was inventing to meet her desire of how the world should be. I saw right through it. I agreed with the 'why' but the actual concept was wrong. Today's class made it clear what she was doing. She was blending the line. She was trying to create a narrative to support the truth that she wants out in front. She's dangerous."

"As they say, power corrupts. Absolute power, corrupts absolutely, and with that in mind, can we get Thai food tonight for dinner?" Sally asked.

"Sounds good," Rachel and Charlie answered.

They spent another hour or so finding where the librarian's line was and discussing whether or not internet sites should be using labels like a library and directing traffic as such.

CHAPTER 33

"You know it's funny. Every night we come here to study and I don't think I have ever really thought about what this place is and what it represents."

"Sounds like you are tugging pretty hard on a thread there," responded Sally jokingly.

Sally was the logical methodical one. She rarely reacted with high emotion and came across as cold. Rachel and Charlie accepted and loved her for this.

Rachel was the fiery one. Her purpose was to find flaws in the arguments and positions of others and to help those in need. It was how she was wired. On many nights, Charlie and Sally found themselves in tow behind Rachel as she walked through the village, knowing exactly where to go and greeting and feeding the homeless, the needy and the strays. All seemed to warm to her instantly while some brustled or shifted their gaze away from the others.

Charlie was the philosopher and thinker. His brain moved a mile a minute and rarely stopped even when sleeping as the two women knew. Regularly, he would wake them up in the middle of the night with a big idea or an epiphany that hit him like a snowball on a wintry day. Bam.

"Think about this place. I think we need to do some research on the history of libraries and librarians. I'll set the alarm. Go."

When the alarm beeped at ten minutes the three looked up at each other in the second floor study room of the library overlooking the quad, shook their heads 'no' and Charlie set the alarm for another ten minutes. A thread had been pulled that needed more time and attention to process and arrive at some conclusions.

"Sorry. I didn't think the research would be that long," Charlie said after the third alarm chimed

"Yeah. Wow. To think that the history of this room goes so far back. I guess I assumed libraries were a product of American history with Ben Franklin and John Dewey at the forefront. Those two barely made a contribution," stated Sally.

"It's crazy to me how many things I have put on the list of 'created by Americans' only to find out that the lessons taught to me were just stories and narratives to paint the USA in a brighter light. Weird," answered Rachel.

"Yeah, right," agreed Charlie.

"To think this place is here because of Egypt before Chrst is certainly not what I was expecting. I assumed libraries were a product of western civilization." Rachel went on, "I remember in high school my first experience like this. We had a funny teacher. I forget his name but he was from Fes in Morocco. It was sophomore year and around September 11th. We were discussing it and many in the class hated all Muslims for the attack. They were brought up to believe all Muslims were bad and had been our mortal enemies throughout history.

"So we are in the middle of this lesson, the haters were saying things like 'teach, you are fine but all other Muslims want to kill us'. He took the insults and hate of his religion for ten minutes or something. Then, I remember this with such clarity, he sat at his desk silently for a few minutes plotting while methodically folding and tearing paper. Then he stood and handed one to each student.

"Pop quiz," he said. "One question. 100 points."

Some of the class booed while others cheered. I just watched. I knew a curveball was being thrown our way.

"Again. Pop quiz. One question. 100 points. When you are finished, flip the paper over and put it in the right hand corner of your desk for me to collect. The only thing I ask is to be quiet for the next 3-4 minutes. Ok?"

The class agreed and he wrote the question on the board. 'What country was the first country to recognize America as a free and sovereign nation and no longer under the colonial rule of Great Britain?'

"I had guessed France because of the Statue of Liberty. Many of the students with Latino backgrounds picked Spain. Some picked Germany or Italy.

"He walked around the room. I wish I could remember his name. It's on the tip of my tongue but it is not important. Flipping over and looking at each answer saying wrong, wrong, wrong. After he had said wrong 38 times, he took his seat and said, 'That was easy to grade. A class of zeroes.'"

The class erupted and he laughed along while quieting the class down before saying, "I knew you didn't know the answer based on how you think about Muslims. You see them as others and not as friends when in fact, the Muslim Kingdom of Morocco was the first nation to recognize you nation, America, as free and sovereign and no longer owned and ruled by Great Britain."

"From that moment on, I started to question everything. I could no longer accept answers at face value especially when they painted one group or another in a dim or bad light. Just think about librarians. We see them as these old weird people who tell us to be quiet around books but that's not who they are. That's who we have been taught to think they are. That libraries and librarians are expendable. We have Google and Wikipedia," finished Rachel.

"Yeah. That's not who they are. They are the guardians of truth. Franklin and Dewey just made their roles more understandable and accessible for the common man by separating libraries into fiction and nonfiction. Truth and lies," exclaimed a wired Charlie.

"They should have power and a voice especially now with the truth being on trial almost daily," responded Sally.

They continued their discussion well into the night landing on answers and questions that seemed to bubble to the surface regularly. Life is simple. Why man makes solutions so complex and confusing was their usual stopping point before calling it a night.

"My brain is cooked," Sally said.

"Mine too," responded Charlie.

"Home?" asked Rachel.

The three nodded and left the second floor study room of the library overlooking the quad and headed home together.

CHAPTER 34

As the semester ticked away, it was obvious even to himself that Donald was having a hard time. Usually cock sure, he was now frequently filled with self-doubt. Even his appearance had changed from clean shaven and well groomed to unkempt.

"Terry, I just don't get it. In high school I was the king of the world. Here, I am a fly on the wall but only on boring walls. Do you know I haven't gotten laid in two months? Two months."

"Sorry man. I am sure it will turn around. You are just in a rut," responded Terry.

But Terry wasn't so sure. When he had met and paired up with Donald for Styles's class, he himself had been at a low point. Yet, with more and more frequency he was finding some success. He had landed a girlfriend, Janice, who seemed to align well with his future and he was having sex a few days a week. She was his first and now his regular. He was flying high which made it harder to deal with the constant bemoans of Donald.

Donald's struggle was real and was enabled by his parents who doted on him. They never gave him clear advice. Just unbridled support and love. It bugged him because he didn't know where to turn. He could feel Terry pulling away and understood why but couldn't figure out how to get off of the train.

"Donald, please stay after class for a minute," Styles suggested after a near public breakdown of Donald over the topic of Star Trek vs Star Wars. It was usually a class the students responded to well and had fun with. Donald's response showed he was on the edge.

Styles understood that not all students succeeded and worse yet, survived. He had lost a few over the years to drugs, accidents, sickness and suicide. He vowed to himself he would help where he could and not blame himself when he couldn't. College students were adults but even the brightest and smartest adults needed support.

"Let's take a walk. I'll give you a pass for your next class and square it with your teacher if that is alright?"

"Sure," answered Donald and they walked out of the main academic building onto the quad.

The campus was beautiful especially in the fall with oaks, pines and a huge weeping willow off to one corner of the quad that offered shade when shade was needed. The reds of the brick complemented the reds, oranges and yellows of the trees and the greens left those seeing them at peace. There was something natural and mystic about seeing the color green in nature. It tells the backbrain that nature is well and teeming with life.

The pair walked towards the dining hall and stopped at the second picnic bench guarding the entrance.

"Take a seat. Donald. Can I get you a coffee or tea?"

"Coffee would be nice."

As Styles walked into the dining hall, Donald felt unsure. This was a weird and a first experience for him. Hanging out with a teacher outside of class. This was not what he had expected when Styles had called on him.

Styles had learned from a fellow teacher and mentor, Paul Sandlin, that when you needed to have a difficult conversation with a student, it was best over a drink, non-alcoholic of course. It forced the student to stay and hear what needed to be said. He had adapted the idea to a hot drink. It needed to cool, giving a few maybe needed moments longer for the talks.

"Here you go, Donald."

"Thanks. Cheers."

"I will go out on a limb here and say that I am not your all-time favorite teacher, especially since our first after class meeting in my office."

Donald agreed. He hadn't even realized that the only other time they had spoken face to face was over the essay that he had written and had received a less than exemplary grade. It made his blood boil a little to think about it and now wondered why he had accepted the offer of coffee.

"What? Is my writing not up to par again?"

"No. Your writing is fine, Donald. I expect you will earn an A for the semester, but no, that is not why I brought you here. I'll get to it. Every year there are a few students who have a hard time. The honeymoon phase of college ends and almost immediately the divorce phase begins. It's a transitional time and the change is always hard for those who change the most."

"What does this have to do with me?"

"I don't know. I have been a teacher for most of my life. I see success and struggle. Your friendship with Terry has helped him out of his shell and now he seems to be happy. But I think that came at a price to you. I think his success changed the dynamic of the friendship. He no longer needs a friend. He now chooses to be your friend."

"And?" Donald answered defensively. He was not liking the conversation or the feelings that were coming to the surface.

"So, when that dynamic changed you lost some of your value to him, like a dip in the stock market. His success came at a cost and it looks like, among other reasons, that the cost was you. You started the year argumentative and cocksure. You now are reserved and distant."

Donald rubbed his eyes. He really did not like where this was going and then went there.

"Can I be honest with you, Professor Styles?"

"Of course. That is why we are here."

"I feel broken. I don't have a direction. I was so used to succeeding. And when I arrived here, I never contemplated failing and now I am failing, or at least feel like I am. Terry is with Janice and I tag along sometimes but it used to be, him following me. I used to be the center and now I am not. It sucks. I don't know. It's almost like I lost myself. I don't know who I am if that makes sense."

By now, Donald was crying and Styles was listening intently and hopeful. When students were open with their feelings and problems, the solutions were easier to come by.

"You saw it at the beginning of class. I was ignored by the Triune, who are attached at the hip, and since then, I have no one except Terry and he spends more and more time with Janice. My friends from last year aren't as responsive to me even in the dining hall when I am grabbing dinner. It's like they don't want to hang out with me."

"Could it be that the last few times you did enter their social scene, you brought a negative vibe? I will tell you this. No one makes it through life without struggle. Struggle is part of life and usually after the struggle the reward is revealed. I have been watching you since the first day of class change. We are being honest here. Today, I could see that your struggle was not just with my class. That there was something else going on up here."

Styles tapped the side of his head and took a sip of coffee. Donald drank too.

"The hard part of sophomore year is that, as I said, the honeymoon is over. You know the school and what it has to offer but you have said no to some activities and offerings that are here for you. You have closed doors by not entering. Do you understand? Last year, your RA and others were there to help you get settled and find your wings or path. You arrived such a big fish from high school that kept you afloat for a year. Now, you are sinking. Is what I am saying making sense?"

"Yes. I remember last year one group went on a weekend canoe trip and another to NYC to see 5 off Broadway plays in two days. I didn't opt to go. There were big parties on those weekends and I stayed to go."

"What would you have done differently?"

"I think I would have gone on the canoe trip. Those who went came back telling stories of their adventure. Probably not the theater. They came back talking weirdly pretending they were other people."

"Okay, let's see what we can do to turn you around a bit. What do you think? Would you like some help?"

"Yes please."

They made a toast with their coffees and then Styles beckoned Donald to follow him. They crossed the quad again past the weeping willow down a stone alleyway to a doorway labeled Outdoor Club.

They entered and Donald was amazed. Past that door was what seemed like another world with bicycles, climbing ropes, paddles, kayaks and canoes littered all over the space and a wall and cave behind the counter where some were climbing up or around fake walls of rock.

"Hey Professor. Are you here to climb today?" asked a slow mouthed student.

"Nope. Not me Ted but this is Donald, I think he could use a lesson."

"Sounds good. Donald, what size shoe do you wear?"

"9.5"

"Here. Try these nines. You want the shoe to fit tight."

Over his years at AU, Styles had brought a few students to the Outdoor Club. He found that those who were the lowest needed to get high quicker so that they would continue climbing or fall down sooner. Ted had been one of those students and now, at the very least, was happy.

Styles watched for a few while Donald and Ted chatted and disappeared behind the counter into the cave.

Over the next few months, Donald's beard became longer and more scraggly. His clothing speckled with chalk and splashes of color either blood or dirt. His waistline thinned. His shoulders broadened. His hands thickened. His smile returned.

CHAPTER 35

Professor Styles grew increasingly aware and increasingly worried about a lump he had discovered in his armpit one morning while applying deodorant. It didn't hurt but he thought it deserved examination.

A call from his doctor inviting him to come back to the office for the results was a sign for the worst. Styles knew that bad news was only given face to face and good news was doled out on the phone so as to not waste time.

Styles arrived at the doctor's office the following morning at 9am sharp after a sleepless night. The room was sterile and white which was in stark contrast to the black receptionist sitting behind the desk and the black doctor standing by her side. It seemed surreal.

"Good morning Professor Styles," said Dr. Eric Owuso.

"Good morning Eric."

"Can I get you a coffee or tea?"

"Coffee would be nice. Thank you."

"Two coffees please for Professor Styles and one for me," Owusa asked the receptionist before beckoning Styles to follow him down the corridor to his office.

After the coffee was brought and formalities finished, Owusa got down to business.

"You are not dumb Professor so I am sure you know that I did not just bring you here for a morning coffee and conversation."

"I had thought not."

"So let me cut through the pretense and straight to the matter. You have a malignant lump closing in on your heart. If we do not remove it, you will die. The good news is that it is still operable and that the chance of success is high. The bad news is that the window is closing. We would need to start treatment immediately. Knowing you as I do, I would assume that would be a difficult choice this time of the school year. You would not finish out your classes."

"I see," Styles answered, not really surprised. "Thank you for not beating around the bush. You know me well Eric but not that well.."

They laughed like they did often and had many times over the years. Eric Owusa and Styles had met the year before Styles had been hired to teach at AU. He had been traveling through Africa along the east coast by bike and had met Eric at the hostel he had stayed at in Ghana where he landed after getting a flat. They had become fast friends.

Over the course of an evening and maybe one too many beers, Eric had confided that he was HIV+ and gay.

"You see being a gay man in Ghana is not good. I am not allowed to be free. Being a gay man with HIV in Ghana is not good at all. I have to hide."

"I see," said Styles and thought about what it must be like to live in fear time two.

They spent the next week chatting all things worldly with Owusa asking questions that helped him paint a picture of the world outside Ghana and providing answers that demonstrated his keen mind and his gift to think and learn. It was why when he had been offered the position at AU, he had one special request.

"Dean, without hesitation, I accept the position at AU and will do my best to help build its legacy for Gloria, the future and for us. I will do my best here. I do have one special request."

Styles went on to tell the Dean about Owusa and after some strings being pulled, Eric had a brand new passport in hand, a student visa and a friend waiting to pick him up from JFK airport in NY when he landed.

Owusa had graduated the top of his class and had gone onto the PhD program at Johns Hopkins University where he also graduated at the top of his class and to the dismay of the hospital had turned down positions offered to him to return to AU as the primary care physician of the school. He had found a new home. One that loved and accepted him and he felt he had no reason to find another.

"When would you recommend for me to begin treatment?"

"I was thinking that this afternoon. Would that give you enough time to get your work in order? Your house of course will be taken care of by Kisi and me."

Like Styles, Owusa had made one request of the dean when accepting the physician's position, that a similar opportunity would be made available for his only sister Kisi. This wish had been granted and upon graduation, she had partnered with her brother as his assistant at the clinic doing what was needed. That morning she had been at the receptionist's desk.

"I don't see that being enough time Eric. Will tomorrow be fine?"

Styles knew Eric well. He knew that Kisi and he would continue to take care of his home despite his protests. He also understood clearly what was being said between the lines. His diagnosis was worse than he was being led to believe and that sooner rather than later would make a difference.

"Tomorrow afternoon will be fine and to think I was worried that you would argue."

"Eric, I may love my students and want to do my best by them but I cannot do my best in the realm we go to next."

"I agree and it will be my pleasure to take care of you. I will see you here tomorrow at 12 to begin treatment and to explain what the next few months will entail."

Styles shook Owusa's hand and that ended their doctor appointment.

"I am sorry that you are sick, Professor Styles. I will do my best to fix you."

"I know you will, Eric."

They hugged and Styles left the office walking back down the corridor to reception where Kisi met him with a bright smile and sad eyes. They said their goodbyes and Styles walked out into his last day of freedom for a while.

CHAPTER 36

Spring on campus was a beautiful sight. The trees bloomed. Green became the prevalent color over winter grey. Life seemed to come back from some form of human hibernation. Lighter shoes. Less clothing. More movement. Like the whole campus was suddenly awoken from a depression and all those depressed suddenly had a hop in their step. Or maybe this was just what he was thinking while he crossed campus for maybe his last time.

"Good morning class."

"Good morning Professor Styles."

Styles liked that the return 'good morning' had occurred organically as a response to his. He had heard many professors and teachers complain about not receiving even a modicum of respect.

"Class will be short today and I will get to the point. I received some unpleasant news yesterday. I was diagnosed with cancer that cannot wait to be treated."

A collective gasp was heard and then the class fell silent.

"Later today, under the care of my doctor, I will begin treatment. That treatment will keep me away from class until I recover, which may or may not be by the end of the school year. I am sorry."

After meeting with Owusa, Styles had gone directly to the Dean.

"Good morning Rosa. Is the Dean in?"

"Good morning Professor. May I ask what this is regarding?"

"It is of a private and urgent nature or I would have made an appointment."

Rosa picked up her phone and dialed the Dean's extension and then pointed to the door.

"Good morning Professor Styles. To what do I owe the honor?"

Styles was one never to mince words and also sometimes preferred the theatrical. "Cancer," he answered.

The dean responded with silence and a welcoming gesture to the leather couch by the door where Styles sat and the Dean took a perch on the matching leather chair next to it.

"I see. What do you know thus far and what do you need from me and the AU community?"

"An hour ago Doctor Owusa diagnosed me with a rather rare form of cancer that if untreated soon, will attack my heart and lungs and prove fatal so he wants to start treatment including a surgery as soon as possible. He suggested today. I said we could wait until tomorrow."

The Dean rose from her desk and picked up her phone to speak with Rosa about a replacement for Styles and what teachers were available for those times. Given technology, the process only took a few strokes of the keys instead of hours of referencing and cross-referencing.

"Are you sure, Rosa?"

"Can you please check again? Maybe add another filter."

Styles and Dean Yoltas rarely minced words, preferring to cut to the chase. It was why Styles was apprehensive when Yoltas sat back down, clearly choosing her next words wisely.

Yoltas took a moment to stare out the window. Hiring Westford had been a mistake and Yoltas knew it. She just had no way of removing her unless an egregious error was made and reported. Until then, no action could be taken. In academia, this was the catch 22. It was hard for students to go against teachers even when the teachers were in the wrong because the teacher wielded the power of the grade and the student's reputation.

"Sometimes when the bough breaks, the levy falls. This seems to be the case and I am sorry. The only person available to take your place is Professor Westford and given your history, I know that this is not welcome news."

The class had begun shuffling again with sound waiting in anticipation for the news as to who would replace Professor Styles for the rest of the semester. When he announced the name Glory Westford not a breath of air was taken or was a sound made while Styles gathered his things and left class for the day.

When the door had shut behind Styles, Donald was the first to speak. "Fuck."

The class collectively laughed and moaned simultaneously in tradition with the mission of AU to be inbetween.

"She is a witch."

"Awful."

"I hate her."

"What should we do?"

"My grades will tank."

Rachel took the lead and spoke next. The class devised a plan that would allow them to continue learning while collectively standing together as a force against Westford. Making it impossible for her to take the power away from the students that had been given to them by Styles.

CHAPTER 37

Westford was liked by few and respected by less. She believed in the ivory tower and it is where she dwelled looking down from her perch on those she perceived as being below her. She treated her colleagues with an air of detachment and others around her as inferior. There was no other way to put it.

She had grown up in a nameless state in a nameless town with nameless schools and a somewhat racist mascot. She had been top of her class and had been awarded a full academic scholarship to the nameless state school where she had graduated in the middle of her class with both a bachelors and masters in education. From there she went to work at the high school she had graduated from while taking night classes to earn her PhD in Education.

She was a woman of little substance and a knack for selling herself as something more when the time was right. Her letter of references were always written by her and signed by the sender. Her resume was up to date and dotted all the Is and crossed all the Ts usually garnering her, at very least, a callback of interest whether it was at a position she was applying for or a conference in which she wanted to speak.

Westford was an elitist snob of no merit and knew this to be true spending hours a week hiding the fact. It was why, when asked by Dean Yoltas to cover for Professor Styles while he was out, she jumped on the chance, agreeing a moment too quickly.

"Professor Styles will be out for the foreseeable future for personal reasons starting tomorrow afternoon. I need you to cover two of his classes including the 'History of Ideas' if you can."

"Anything I can do for the school, you know that I will. I would be glad too."

The Dean knew in the response that something was up. A train had just pulled out of the station heading for a wreck and there was nothing she could do about it. All she could do was hand Westford the lesson plans that Styles had left her and wish for the best.

That night the Triune met in the top right room of the library overlooking the quad.
"I am going to ask about it. Do you think Prof Styles will survive and be back by the end of the school year?" Charlie questioned.

"I don't know," said Sally, staring out the window watching dark shadows cross the quad.

"Me neither. But I am so screwed if he doesn't. Westford hates me and I mean hates. We had it out with the Dean a few months ago. I can't stand her and how she treats others and worse yet, she's a knowitall fraud," responded Rachel.

"So what is the plan? What can we do? I wouldn't mind taking the class again but only with Styles. It would be hell to have to take it a full year with her just to graduate."

They spent the rest of the night devising a way to eliminate Westford, going so far as to thinking about hiring an assassin, trying to seduce her and to catch her committing fraud as an intellectual. They chose the latter. None were okay with murder and none wanted to sleep with her no matter the outcome.

CHAPTER 38

An email pinged the class, Dean Yoltas and Dr. Westford. The heading was simple. It read today's assignment for class.

Yoltas opened the email and laughed, spilling coffee on her blouse forcing her to change it before work. There was only one question. 'Why can war be justified?' Explain. Yoltas already knew that trouble was brewing on the horizon. Styles was a revered teacher. Westford was not. She was tolerated as a means to an end by the students that was all. Few fell under her good graces.

Styles did not. He knew it. Westford knew it. Yoltas knew it. This email would cause a kerfuffle. The topic of Dr. Westford's PhD was why war is justifiable.

By the time Yoltas returned from her wardrobe with a new blouse another email had arrived. This time from Westford. In the subject heading it read Urgent and the body read that she was insulted beyond belief and that the Dean needed to do something about it immediately.

Yoltas did. She responded to the email by stating that they could discuss the matter in more detail after the class which was set to start in 30 minutes at 8:30.

At 10:30 Westford was shown into the dean's office.

"Can you believe the gaul of Styles? He undermined and insulted me on purpose in front of the students and you."

"I take it the class didn't align with you."

"No, they did not. Furthermore, it is unprofessional what he did."

"What was unprofessional? To assign work to his class that aligns with his curriculum. I can see why you are frustrated but no, I do not see it as unprofessional. It was a jab and insulting but not unprofessional. He was working within the confines of his position. That is all."

"I can't believe this. I just spent two hours under fire with children telling me that I was wrong. I will not stand for this."

"Again, I see your frustration but you could have handled it differently."

Yoltas rarely blew up and even more rarely, did so in front of others. She had become Dean because of her even keel personality. One that was analytical, could see both sides of an argument and the flaws of both sides in a New York minute. Rarely, if ever, did she take sides. She lived by the ethos that just because one side believes they are right does not mean that the other side is wrong. That was foolish thinking. Both, in fact, could be right and both wrong.

"Sit down Dr. Westford. I do not like when others stand above me. It is not becoming of someone who survives by earning power."

Wesford sat down and then said, "Are you telling me I don't do my job well?"

"I am telling you this and I will be frank. I will also record this conversation for later use so that you can peruse it at your leisure. I do not want my words to be mistaken."

Yoltas opened an app on her phone and pressed record.

"Dr. Westford, some of what I may say may seem offensive. It is not meant to be. These are criticisms that in the past I have sugar coated hoping that you would read between the lines and change. It is obvious that a hand's off take responsibility for yourself approach is not going to work. So let me clear the day. We hired you because of your letters of reference, Linkedin profile, resume and cover letter. You came across as a wonderful choice. Since then, the wool has been ripped off the school's eyes including mine but not limited to me."

Westford squirmed in her chair before standing and stating, "I do not have to take this."

"Sit down!" demanded Dean Yoltas. "If you walk out that door, I will take it as your resignation. Do I make myself clear?"

Westford slunk back into her seat.

"It is clear to me that you are magnificent at painting and selling a wonderful picture of yourself. It is also clear that the picture and the reality are very different. Students complain about you regularly to me, to each other and on online forums and other staff complain or trash talk you behind your back. Your teacher ratings are the lowest in the school. I have not looked to compare you with other teachers at other schools. I do not have the time or interest. So, I will tell you this, if I were you, I would look at fixing your problems.

"Now, to the issue at hand. Yes, Professor Styles sent an email that I am sure he knew would rub you the wrong way. but it was also within his rights as the teacher of record for the class. You are an adult. Your immediate response this morning and this one demonstrates an inability to see things from a different point of view. This goes against the very principles by which the school was founded. Duplicity is our motto. That there is not one way, but simultaneously two or more paths to choose and take.

You do not exemplify this in your teacher persona here. Students complain regularly that you teach them that it is your way or the highway. Well, we may get to the highway, but not for them, for you.

"So I will leave it at this, if I get a complaint from a student or group of students about how you are teaching, I will no longer try to diffuse the situation but use it as a stepping off point to set in motion your dismissal. Do I make myself clear?"

Westford was sweating. She wanted to rip off her jacket and shirt to get air. She felt like she was suffocating and she knew that if she pushed, she would lose. She had had similar conversations with both of her previous bosses and had changed long enough to change positions and be hired somewhere new so that her issues could be swept under the rug. She knew that she had just hit a dead end.

"What do you suggest?" Westford asked with a tad of condescendence.

"I would suggest that you learn to be more open to the difference of opinions of others and to not take issue when someone doesn't agree or something doesn't go your way. Either grow a thicker or a slicker skin. Or both.

"Now, I understand that the question Professor Styles asked got your goat. You have every right to be ticked, but the primary purpose and goal of that class is to think outside of what you or I or anyone else may think. It is about seeing beyond the box that we have put ourselves in and to explore the edges and just beyond giving the students the reins to create the solutions for their future. Not ours."

Yoltas continued by asking, "Do you know what one of the first lessons Professor Styles teaches?"

"No, I have not audited his class and have no interest in the man," Westford responded curtly.

"He discusses change and how change has a ripple effect and that we accept it only as going forward but rarely examine its effects going backwards. For example, the sky. It was once a piece of cloth separating heaven and Earth. It is clearly not but all ideas up until that moment of discovery were based on that fact indirectly at least. That is what I want you to think about. You may be right about all. I am not a judge but try to be open to being wrong. That would be my advice to you. It may make your life easier. If there is nothing else, I have to be across campus in 15 minutes for a meeting with the board of trustees."

"No. That is all."

Westford rose from her seat and exited the Dean's office. The Dean pressed stop on her phone and emailed the recording to herself, HR and Westford. If a storm was brewing, she wanted to be prepared.

CHAPTER 39

As Ted introduced Donald to climbing and other outdoor activities, Donald wondered where he was. Sure he had seen climbing in the movies and TV but that was for others. He was into baseball, which he wasn't very good at, and basketball which he could play well enough. American sports. Climbing and skateboarding seemed designed for a different breed of man, the outsiders and outcasts.

So to find himself in this weird industrial cave space was unfamiliar and as Ted showed him literally how to use the ropes, different hand movements for grips and different toe holds, Donald found himself enjoying the changes within and fighting them with every fiber of his being. He was living on a border.

One change was to his physique. He had never been fat but climbing burned through so many calories that he quickly trimmed down to sinew and only muscles needed to climb. In the few months since the day Styles introduced him to Ted, Donald's life was back on track. His grades shot up and for one of the first times in his life, he was happy due to his own accord.

Donald had even graduated to climbing real rock outside and was unsure about it. Indoor climbing seemed safer like flying seemed safer in a plane than with a hang glider.

"On belay," yelled Ted.

"Belay is on," Donald yelled back.

"Climbing."

Climb on."

And Donald watched Ted climb the second pitch of two up Directissima, a 5.9. A bit above Donald and a few steps below Ted.

In the gym Donald had become fascinated by Ted. He was this lanky awkward guy with a few pimples, shaggy hair, a hawk nose and two unmatching lips. To Donald, at first glance, Ted was a weirdo. But once he donned his climbing shoes, chalked his hands and started to move, there was no other way to describe him other than economically graceful. Each move was fluid. His calloused hands were strong and his forearms veiny as was his neck when he went for a hard move or got excited when speaking.

Donald climbed with a fury so as to be seen as, at the very least, competent in Ted's eyes, and in the few months they had known each other had become fast friends. When Ted had invited Donald for a weekend trip to the Shawgunks in New Paltz, New York, he had agreed immediately.

When Donald made it to the top of the second pitch Ted asked, "So what did you think?"

"Never thought I would see myself climbing up a wall just to see a view as beautiful as this. Wow."

"I agree. I am glad Styles introduced us. He seems to really get his students. He's different from all my others."

"Agreed, but I did not like him at first. He didn't teach the way I was used to learning so I thought he was awful. I was wrong. I thought he hated me. That day we met. I was lower than low and here I am taller than tall." And then Donald bellowed to hear the echo of his voice and Ted followed suit. "Ohooooo!"

After climbing, Donald and Ted headed back down and set up camp for the night. As they got ready for bed, Donald saw Ted taking off his shirt and realized it was the first time he had ever seen Ted's bare torso.

Donald was not an exhibitionist but went with the flow and in the climbing gym, many others climbed topless once they were warmed up. Even the women would unrobe and climb only in their sports tops or bras.

As Donald examined Ted's torso he could see a red line from his shoulder running into his chest.

"What happened, if you don't mind me asking?" Donald questioned pointing to his own shoulder while looking at Ted's.

"Not at all," Ted responded while quickly putting his shirt back on. "This," he pointed to his shoulder, "is a reminder to not get in the car with a drunk driver ever."

Ted had grown up in the South, the son of self described hillbillies. They played the part so well that they even brewed their own moonshine and rarely took interest in the kids that they were tripping over as they brewed and drank and repeated the process.

From the first day of school Ted understood very clearly that if he wanted out of the town and a similar fate, he needed to use school as a stepping stone to a brighter future. He worked diligently becoming the top student with not much effort or fuss and spent hours erasing his southern drawl so that strangers would not immediately judge him.

He grew up in Northern Mississippi in Appalachia. The mountains had always been his home and being outdoors and climbing were now his only remaining connections to his home.

"I grew up in Mississippi. I've told you that before but I don't think I have painted a clear picture. I grew up in the Appalachian mountains of Mississippi in a corner of the state that only those that live there have reason to know and remember. My parents were good folk but also moonshiners and drug dealers. That's what they did. Organic was their game. They sold drugs that were in their minds 'natural' like mushrooms, marijuana, cocaine and moonshine, not meth or PCP which is a good thing or I don't think my mind would have developed as well as it did."

"Crazy. That's so far removed from mine. Like the polar opposite."

"I have gathered; it's why I haven't shared. I don't keep it hidden but I don't share it publicly. I don't want their lives to influence my future."

"I get it. What about the scar?"

"Yeah. I got chickenpox and my parents were called to pick me up from school. I guess my dad thought he was sober enough to drive. He made it to the school and I went out to meet him at the car and we were off. I was in 6th grade. A week later I woke up in a hospital with a rebuilt shoulder, a healing concussion and no more dad. He had rolled the truck into a ravine and didn't make it. I did. This is a reminder of him."

"Wow."

Donald and Ted set a small fire and cooked some dinner before retiring into their tent. They shot the shit for a while longer before going to sleep. When they woke up, they packed up camp and went back to the wall for another day of hardscrabble climbing.

Before hitting the wall again, Ted removed his shirt no longer self-conscious with Donald or his history.

"On belay," said Ted.

"Belay is on."

"Climbing."

"Climb on."

Donald was in a trance watching Ted climb. Each muscle in his back was working while he moved up the rock wall while Donald tried to keep pace with the ropes. It was a site to see. This gangly awkward looking boy who climbed with such grace.

When it was Donald's turn, he did not fare so well. The climb was a 5.10 and a few moves were beyond his ability. He inwardly promised to himself that he would improve so that he could master this route on their next trip which he hoped would be soon.

CHAPTER 40

Later that night, after climbing a few shorter routes and taking a hike in the woods, Donald and Ted made it back to camp for dinner and another night's sleep in the tent under the stars.

Donald knew that climbing had ups and downs. He had changed as a young man because of it. He had become self aware and less self absorbed. Life was a process not a destination like his parents believed and had conditioned him to think. He preferred this new version better than the old one especially in the mirror when his toned abs, shredded shoulders and strong legs were in view.

During dinner Ted was noticeably quieter than normal. He had had two hard days of climbing and was enjoying the time outside and away from buildings and life like he had done so often as a child.

"Man, I hope I can make that move someday. That heel hook to a pincher to a decent hold combo looks so easy when you do it but impossible to me when I am on the wall."

"It's a bugger alright. You really need to stay close to the wall and keep your weight balanced. That's it. Remember the orange route at the gym the first day you were there. That first move was the problem. That took you two weeks to get. This one you will get on your next trip. I am sure of it."

"You're probably right," answered Donald.

"I am going to turn in. We have to wake up early to get back in time for classes."

With that Ted got up and headed into the tent leaving Donald by himself which was uncharacteristic of them. They had become close friends joined at the hip when they could find time to climb or hang out together.

Donald climbed into the tent soon after.

"You alright, Ted?"

Ted didn't answer.

"Come on. What gives?"

Again silence.

"Come on. We are having a great time. What's up?"

Donald could see Ted thinking and wanting to speak but stopping and trying and stopping again until he took a deep breath and blurted out, "I am gay."

Now it was Donald's turn to be silent. He just stared across the tent at Ted for a few moments while Ted stared back at him.

"I am gay. I am a homo from the south. So what? It shouldn't matter. Should it? I mean it's 2022. Who cares? Right? One in ten people are gay. I am just one of the ones. It shouldn't matter. And yes, it means I am attracted to men, not women. It's part of who I am and I am sorry if it bothers you but I needed you to know."

Donald had never been around someone openly gay until coming to AU. It was eye-opening and intense. He had grown up in a conservative state in a conservative town with conservative parents attending a conservative church. He was programmed that being gay was wrong if not a sin in as many words.

When he arrived at AU and saw that many of his classmates and neighbors in the dorms were exploring their bi-sexuality or openly gay, it was a shock to Donald. He had always been straight and attracted to girls. That was part of who he was and as the idea appeared and lingered in his head, he came full-stop on the word 'was'. The Donald that had arrived two years ago at AU was not the same Donald that was sitting across from Ted.

"Can I see that scar again on your shoulder?"

Ted took off his shirt.

Donald traced his hands over the scar, mesmerized by it and feeling electric from the touch. Then the moment came as it does. Eyes connecting. Gravity pulling each other together for a kiss. Neither hesitated.

Ted was the first to speak. "I am gay but that was my first kiss. Maybe we should take it slow."

"I have been gay for two minutes. Slow seems like the right pace."

They both laughed. Kissed again and went to sleep, hands embraced in the tent under the stars knowing that neither would get a good night's sleep but the price to pay to satisfy their wants would be too great and would undo their needs and the sinew that was binding them together.

CHAPTER 41

The Trifecta sat in silence in the second floor library study room overlooking the quad. None could find words to speak. They just knew that being in each other's company was where they wanted to be and what Professor Styles would want. For thinking to carry on.

There was not an alarm in the center of the room. There was no frenetic energy as each tried to uncover some truth over a topic new or old. There were no clicks of keyboards or mouses sending them to places far and wide. There was no pen scratch on paper as interesting tidbits of data were found. The Trifecta was just there. Sitting silently in the second floor library study room overlooking the quad. Inert. For the first time together they were being and doing nothing more.

Sally was the first to go. She broke the silence by sliding her chair backwards with a screech, standing which moved the air from stagnant to circulating, collected her things and walked out.

Charlie followed and then Rachel.

Back at home, Sally greeted the two at the door with a smile and kiss to both.

"I didn't and don't know what to say but I couldn't bear the silence anymore."

"I understand. Me neither. I just didn't know what to say or how to start."

"Me too. That room is our safe place because Styles brought us together. It seems wrong to be there while he is sick and at the clinic," said Rachel.

Then the Ah-Ha moment hit. The three searched each other's eyes for a moment and then they just laughed. The type of laugh that breaks the pain of stress and then the three walked out the door to go visit Styles.

"Good evening Nurse. We have a weird request. Is there anyplace here that we could set up shop and study while Professor Styles is recovering?"

Nurse Osa greeted the Trifecta and said, "I was told the three of you would arrive. Welcome." She beamed. I am Osa, the sister of Eric Owusa, the physician of Professor Styles and like you, a student of his as well. It is a pleasure to meet you. He will be fine. My brother will give him the best of care and God will do the rest."

The three were mesmerized as this beautiful African woman greeted them with nothing but love and compassion in an honest tone that none had ever heard before.

"The professor is asleep. You are welcome to see him when he awakes. I will come for you when he is up. In the meantime, you have studies to attend to. The second room down the hall to the right is the conference room. You may continue your studies there."

And with that, she put her head down and started clicking on keys letting the three know that the conversation was over and that, while they may be standing idle in front of her, she was not. A small upturn of her lips could be seen as the three looked at each other amazed and then headed down the hall to the second room on the right.

"Good evening," a man in a white coat said as he rose to greet them. "I am Doctor Eric Owusa and I am a friend and a student of Professor Styles and have been one for many years. Welcome to your new temporary study space."

The night before, Eric, Osa and Marc had eaten together. During dinner, after the discussion of the upcoming treatment, Marc had brought to attention a concern.

"This year, like some years before, I have some students who are exemplary. Like you and Osa. They are a team and I think they may also be lovers, but I do not know. I do know that they work together and do so in such a way that I hope my being sick does not interfere."

"Why would it?" asked Osa.

"The three, or Trifecta as they are known, work in the study room above the library overlooking the quad. They are there often and are there to learn and pull threads. On the few occasions I have stopped by, I have been impressed, only once or twice willing to cross the room's threshold and enter for fear of disrupting their work."

"So what can we do to help you help them?" asked Owusa.

"I am afraid that being sick will throw them for a loop. They may not be able to stay focused on the now. Instead, they will worry about me."

Owusa bellowed and outlined a plan, that after being explained, left the night open to a myriad of other more pressing problems to be discussed.

"We have been expecting you. I presume? Let me see. It is obvious that you are Charlie. And you must be the runner with your logoed outfit which means that you are Rachel. Welcome. This is now your new space until Professor Styles recovers or you decide to go back to the library."

"Thank you," a shocked Rachel stammered.

"Who are you?" asked Sally.

"I thought I would introduce myself. I am Dr. Eric Owusa of Ghana and friend and student of Professor Marc Styles. We met many years ago in my home village while he was traveling through by bicycle. He had had a flat tire and I had had the privilege of being there to help him. He returned the favor tenfold and here we are. I am forever in his debt and do what I can when he needs. I thought this would be a fitting place for you to study. He is sleeping next door and when he awakes, he will be joyful to learn that the three of you are here and working."

The Trifecta was left speechless again. Twice in one day.

"Where the Professor and I differ in our thinking is over God. So I will ask the question this evening for you to ponder. Does God help healing?" and with that he shook their hands with a smile and beaming eyes and walked out of the second room down the hall on the left leaving the three tasked with work.

CHAPTER 42

Charlie was usually cocksure. Styles being sick had sent him for a loop. He was having a hard time focusing and plodding along like he normally did. Head first. He was aimless.

Sally immersed herself in her running. It was where she had found solace as a child and was a safe place for her to go now, spending more time at the track than with Rachel and Charlie.

Rachel, on the other hand, was handling things well. Once she warmed up to the new surroundings, she was keen on examining them and those that had created them. She adapted quickly.

"Did you know that Owusa and Ola were the first two in their family ever to leave their village, let alone get an education and move away? That's so cool," shared Rachel.

"Really?" asked Charlie.

"Yeah, and Owusa graduated from med school with honors but chose to open up shop here to be closer to Styles. Talking with them this afternoon waiting for you two gave me hope. Is that weird?" asked Rachel.

"No," Sally answered. "I don't think it's weird at all. Think about a funeral or wake. We go to these places to feel a connection with others to the dead. It's why people go. You are just adapting to change better than me and Charlie."

"And Styles ain't dead so there's another positive," interjected Charlie.

Throughout their friendship, the Trifecta usually seamlessly transitioned easily from ups and downs, joy and sadness, to what tied them together, a search for truth. Somewhere in their back brains, they understood that their time was fleeting.

Charlie set his phone on the table and simply stated three words. Funerals. Traditions. Go. The three set off at a feverish pace to explore what they could find.

After the alarm pinged and they started to gather their thoughts, there was a knock on the door followed by the bright smile of Owusa.

"Professor Mark Styles is awake and ready for visitors this morning. Please follow me."

The Trifecta followed Owusa into the hall to the first room on the right marked Patient Room #1. The doctor opened the door and ushered the three in before closing the door behind them and disappearing down the hall.

Patient Room #1 was what anyone would expect. It was a room with a mechanical medical bed, many machines of different uses, a curtain, a small window that looked out onto a small yard and a picture of two grinning younger men standing behind a bicycle. A younger Owusa and a younger and tanned Professor Styles. At the foot of the bed in what could only be described as a smile added to the room were three chairs in an arc.

"Please sit down," Styles offered. "I hope you are well and don't worry, I will be fine. A few more weeks here under the exemplary care of friends, then back home for a few more and then I should be back in class for the last two or three weeks of the year. That being said. What interesting threads have you pulled?"

After a few awkward moments of silence, Styles spoke again, "I know this was hard on you. That is why you are here and have been daily. I also know that you have been working and not sitting next door meditating and praying for my healthy return. It's not in your nature. So out with it. What have you been working on?"

Silence overcame the room again with each of the three looking at the other until Rachel finally took charge.

"Did you know that Muslims bury their dead in shrouds so that the body can decompose and graveyards then become forests over time?" Rachel blurted out.

The room erupted in laughter with Styles laughing so hard it hurt and all four gasping for air.

Once his breath was caught, Styles responded, "Well that's an ice breaker if I have ever heard one."

They all laughed again. This time not as hard.

"Did you know that in Tibet, they have what is called a Sky Burial? They cut the dead into pieces for the birds to eat to carry the souls closer to heaven?" asked Charlie.

"In many Nordic countries, they carry the bodies to the top of mountains with rivers and streams and send the bodies downstream in small boats and allow nature to reclaim the dead?" responded Sally.

"It is good to remember that life is a cycle moving towards death and new life. Nothing more or less. We are here now. Too many people live in fear of this cycle. Those who 'live' life do not. They experience life on life's terms as have I. Being sick sucks but it is also part of life because without sickness, we would never completely understand or celebrate health. Look at Sally. She is the perfect picture of health. You can see it illuminating out from her. Sick people just don't vibrate at the same frequencies.

It's that simple.

"Now, I must rest. I assure you that I will not die this time around. Owusa and Ola would not allow it being reason number one. So I suggest that you continue continuing on and return to the second floor study room in the library overlooking the quad for it is the home of your collective mind and your inspiration, believe it or not, of all those that walk by and see the three of you working there."

They said their goodbyes and promised to visit soon, leaving Styles in the special care of Owusa and Ola.

"Man. I don't know. I am grateful that guy is our teacher," said Charlie.

"I can tell you this. Not all coaches and teachers are the same. Some support us like Styles and my coach and some try to break us down and force us to think like them."

"Like Westford," Rachel said through gritted teeth hiding a devilish smirk. " I hope she gets hers someday. Anyways, a bottle of wine and pizza tonight?"

That night they shared two bottles of wine, a large vegetarian pizza and each other celebrating their lives as selfish individuals and a symbiotic unified entity that needed all of its parts, even the ones designed only for pleasure.

CHAPTER 43

"Do you think that you need to believe in God for heaven to exist?" Owusa asked.

Styles and Owusa were sitting in patient room number 1 playing chess. Owusa knew that if he didn't keep an eye on the professor, he would not heal as quickly.

"To be honest, my best answer is this. I am not sure if it matters as long as you find purpose and live a life here on Earth that gives at least a few others hope. Then, if there is a doom and gloom God of judgment, you will know where you stand as you wait outside the pearly gates," answered Styles.

Styles was wired to move. As his father would say, he was born with ants in his pants. Rarely did he sit still. As he aged, he needed more breaks and with the dawn of the internet and computers, he was obligated to participate as a lifelong learner as both an employee and user. Bureaucratic red tape existed worldwide and technology seemed to just make more of it.

The positive was that his body, old as he was, still healed quickly. Not at the rapid pace of his youth but certainly at a pace that brought a smile to his face and those around him including Owusa who was both pleased and surprised at the progress Styles was making daily.

"It looks like you will be able to go home and begin fending for yourself next week and the following week you may return to your duties at AU," Owusa said.

They were sitting at the little table and chairs in patient room number one. They were playing chess. The day's light created a crisp clean look with hard edges.

"Oh, and by the way. Checkmate," Owusa chuckled after moving his knight.

"I see the student has become the master overnight. That's three for three. It seems you were going light on me over the past few weeks."

Owusa smiled sheepishly and responded, "I wanted to strengthen your positive energies and to rebuild your hope. Now that that is completed, I have resumed playing to my capabilities."

"I see what you have done. One of those little pills must have been designed specially to knock my level of chess down a notch or two just so you could win. I see through your ruse. Now, please give me the antidote."

They both laughed while setting up the board for another game of play. In truth, Styles knew that since their first meeting many years ago and playing chess on the ground in the village in Ghana that he only won when Owusa could tell that Styles was bored of losing so as to keep a partner to play with.

"I don't know," started Sally. "Sometimes I want life to exist as a ladder. Start as birth moving through each station of life until the top rung which is death and the stairway to heaven not to be too cheesy."

Rachel smirked and then responded, "You know that I am not religious so the God question resonates differently to me. I don't feel it so I don't see it or live through it, but I do agree that those with faith seem to have easier access to life and to the top stair of death. I just don't get why so many worry so much about it."

"I think you are on to something," Charlie said. "It's like screen time. The 'religious' spend so much of their gift of life focused on something else. Like someone else's version of 'how life should be'. Anytime I try to go there, my explorer self can't get past go if that makes sense."

"It's almost as if religions are designed as a pacifier to simply pacify and keep us from crying or throwing a tantrum. Imagine what the world would be like without religion? Without rules that blanket all of humanity like snow. Religion and the future concept of heaven are like a down comforter followed by pleasant deep sleep. Who doesn't want to go out that way?"

"But Rachel, if that's the case, why don't we buy in? It seems the stairway to heaven is simply bed, bath and beyond. But we don't. We think and see harm and hate and pain in others."

"And we want to succeed. I do. I run to do my best and hopefully my best has me cross over the finish line first. I don't race in the name of God but I also, if we actually do meet our maker, want it to be proud of me for identifying my gift and using it to the fullest of my ability."

"Yeah Sally, it's strange. I am the same way. I don't want to do harm and sometimes even think that the three of us are doing evil because, not my parents, but certainly the society around me taught me so."

Rachel quipped back. "Maybe we should stop if that's how you feel. I don't want to take part of you winding up in hell for eternity."

"I did not say I wanted to stop. In fact, if it is the highway to hell, I am getting off the stairway."

CHAPTER 44

Rachel entered the second story study in the library overlooking the quad. She dropped her bag on the empty seat next to her left and sat.

"Hey," Charlie said.

"Afternoon," said Sally.

Rachel didn't respond. Sally and Charlie looked at each other with open eyes as to ask if the other knew what was up with Rachel. Both shrugged almost simultaneously. She had left home normally that morning so it must have been something in the last few hours that triggered her silence.

"What gives?" asked Sally after a few minutes of silence had passed.

"I'm so pissed. Westford is a witch."

Since Styles had taken leave, Westford had taken over his class and it was not going well. To add insult to injury, Rachel had another class with Westford. Unfortunately, her reputation had not preceded her far and wide enough before Rachel had enrolled in class.

"What happened?" asked Charlie.

"It's like since she took over Styles' class, she is trying to undermine him by casting shade over his ideas in her other classes. Today, she had the gaul to suggest that ethics was a construct created by those that lead us."

"There's probably some truth in that," Charlie said. "I don't think Styles would take issue with that."

"Then," Rachel continued and Charlie waved a hand of apology for speaking too soon. "The witch went on to say that we should all be more aggressive. That we should be the lion. That we should take what we want and that all that matters is success. She even used herself as an example."

"I hear that all the time at the gym. It's like a new mantra for many athletes, especially the football players. Some of them even chant 'kill, kill, kill' before games," responded Sally.

"But that's not the worst part. The worst part is that she believes success should be achieved at all costs and that those who don't succeed are at fault for not being willing to risk it all."

Rachel held up a finger to illustrate that she was not done and that the worst was yet to come.

"Westford finished by saying, in not so many words, that cheats were still successes. She spent almost two hours justifying that winning by any means possible is the path that we should all be on, especially today with such a huge population, better education globally and more competition. I left sick to my stomach."

"Again, I hear that all the time at the gym. It's the argument between doping and being clean. The debate is not about cutting corners but using all tools available to win. Without winning an athlete doesn't get paid no matter how fit or strong or dedicated they are. It's been hard-wired into the sport industry that doping isn't cheating," responded Sally.

It was Rachel's turn to be dumbfounded and looked at Charlie and then at Sally and then back at Charlie who in return shrugged his shoulders and made a hand gesture stating 'I don't know'.

"Do you dope Sally?" asked Rachel.

"The line between doping and not doping is so grey today as an elite that I don't have that answer. What I do today is legal but one or more of my recovery regiments that I use today may shift to the other side and then I will have to adapt as WADA, the World Anti Doping Administration, shuffles drugs from one column to another and this includes ibuprofen and paracetamol. So, no I don't dope but I do what my coaches prescribe for recovery. In endurance sports, that's the name of the game, and of course, recovery and power to weight ratios. Luckily, genetics and a disdain for sugar and a usual disinterest in bread helps me there. But I wouldn't cross the line to what is illegal. My old coach said to me a long time ago to not build my life on a lie. It resonated with me so I won't but as we all know, the line between lies and truths is sometimes hard to see."

The Trifecta kept on discussing doping in sports and asking questions like whether or not sport is sport and not just sports entertainment if doping and drugs are allowed and whether or not has sport become only an industry that the rich have access to, because now, not only do the athletes need equipment, but also need medical support to succeed. Then they returned to the topic at hand.

"So do you think that success by all means possible is right?" asked Rachel.

"No, I don't but I think many believe those that sell the message. They amass fortunes by cheating and lying, and then build foundations to help others as, maybe, an atonement for their sins. I do know this. Once you begin, it's almost impossible to stop," Sally said.

"It goes back to one of the original questions we asked and

discussed. Is religion a lie or at the very least based on one? If it is, then those who are religious are more willing to accept other lies; it would stand to reason," stated Charlie.

"It's almost like there are two species out there. One, like us, who wants success based on merit and hard work and truth. We think failing is okay. The other sees the arrival at the destination as the only measure of success like Westford. Getting the PhD was the destination. Not learning or thinking or figuring out how her mind and her path and ideas would better humanity," Rachel said.

"It's like one of my favorite quotes 'The Journey is the Reward'. I have always taken that as the truth. You never know what is around the corner. I am a lucky guy for many reasons. One being that I get to wake up with you. I am ever present during our time together because, as we have discussed many times, it is fleeting."

"The three of us live in the now. We celebrate each other and each other's successes. I guess I would just assume that some, like Westford, have had very little support along her path and very few hard won wins. Few mentors or coaches and probably distant parents. She is an old lady who isn't comfortable in her own skin and sells to others that her path is best to make herself feel better about her inner lies and to hide the lies from herself," Sally responded.

"Now, I almost feel bad for her," Rachel stated. "Almost, but no. I think she may in fact be a sad person who needs some help but she is an adult. It is on her to seek help. Not up to us to accept her and her message. She does harm. She's a witch and not a good one."

All students swiped at their phones before breaking out in collective laughter.

"Well played," said Donald. "Brilliant in fact."

"Thanks. I think that just made my year," said Terry.

All students in the class agreed on one thing; that Styles was teaching them and that Westford was not. That her disdain of Styles, which was known throughout the school, had clouded her judgment when proctoring for Styles while he was out.

The night before the Trifecta sent a message to the class. It was simple. It was a clip from the ending of the 1980s movie *The Breakfast Club* in which one student wrote one essay for all. The Trifecta had copied the move. They had written one essay for all and each student printed it out and handed it in with their name as the author. It read as follows:

> *Myths are the building blocks of a functioning society and teach those who learn them how to be good citizens. They reinforce cultural norms and create a thread that all citizens can connect with. That is why a nation is only as strong as its myths which is also why there is only one answer to this question. A culture is only as strong as its stories and those who keep those stories alive.*

> *It is also why students should learn conformity in education and that there is only one answer or path. Free thought creates division. It is only when we think alike with a common purpose that we can succeed and evolve.*

The paper went on for ten more pages to support myths as the building blocks of a functioning society as Westford had lectured.

It was no surprise that later that day the Trifecta found themselves in Dean Yoltas's office.

"I think you know why you are here."

"Yes," the Trifecta answered in unison.

CHAPTER 45

Westford was sitting at the desk at the bottom of the steps in the lecture hall as students started to funnel into class, sitting down and swiping at their phones in the last few moments before the bell. When the bell rang, she began without introduction or preface.

"Professor Styles wanted you to learn about why allegories are used in society. I thought it to be too trite a topic. Instead, you will learn about how a balanced society is based on both truth and lies."

Westford started by telling the class about the three lies that almost all Western childhood was based on: Santa Claus, the Easter Bunny and the Tooth fairy. And that all societies have similar characters. Then, she went on to tell why these three myths are good because they help to breed and build strong citizens who trust their leaders despite their lies like they had their parents. It was the only point made in her two hour lecture that had merit. When she topped it off by stating that it was a patriots duty to teach and support these myths by buying gifts and cards and what not, any positive thread that allowed free thought went out the window.

The caveat or cherry on top was when, at the end of class, she assigned a ten page paper. The topic: Why childhood myths build strong citizens. Then she walked out of the room while the students were left searching for a thread of hope.

When the Trifecta arrived at the top right study room of the library overlooking the quad, they were deflated and disgusted.

"What are we like 12 year olds?" demanded Rachel.

"Who the heck does she think she is?" asked Charlie.

"What a day!" exclaimed Sally.

The study session went on like this for quite some time. They needed to vent. They missed Styles and how he offered ideas, defended his positions and seemed almost gleeful when students proved him wrong or he was proven right. It was dynamic. Being told how to think was what Styles had tried to undo. Westford was trying to put them back in their place. Students under the teacher.

Then the light went on. Two hours later the work was done and their phones pinged with incoming messages of delight.

'Perfect.'

'Well done.'

'Super.'

'Love it.'

Two days later, they arrived at class to find Westford sitting at the bottom of the stairs of the lecture hall with a neat stack of papers in her hand and a grimace on her face.

"This is not what I asked for. You all earned an F."

The class said nothing. Not a word.

"Someone in this room wrote an essay. Then gave it to all the other students to copy. That is cheating plus plagiarism and reason for expulsion. Explain yourself."

The class said nothing.

"I will get to the bottom of this one way or another and then there will be hell to pay," she spit, then grabbed her things and the student essays before storming out of the lecture hall at the top of the stairs with stomping feet and the slamming of the door.

All students swiped at their phones before breaking out in collective laughter.

"Well played," said Donald. "Brilliant in fact."

"Thanks. I think that just made my year," said Terry.

All students in the class agreed on one thing; that Styles was teaching them and that Westford was not. That her disdain of Styles, which was known throughout the school, had clouded her judgment when proctoring for Styles while he was out.

The night before the Trifecta sent a message to the class. It was simple. It was a clip from the ending of the 1980s movie The Breakfast Club in which one student wrote one essay for all. The Trifecta had copied the move. They had written one essay for all and each student printed it out and handed it in with their name as the author. It read as follows:

Myths are the building blocks of a functioning society and teach those who learn them how to be good citizens. They reinforce cultural norms and create a thread that all citizens can connect with. That is why a nation is only as strong as its myths which is also why there is only one answer to this question. A culture is only as strong as its stories and those who keep those stories alive.

It is also why students should learn conformity in education and that there is only one answer or path. Free thought creates division. It is only when we think alike with a common purpose that we can succeed and evolve.

The paper went on for ten more pages to support myths as the building blocks of a functioning society as Westford had lectured.

It was no surprise that later that day the Trifecta found themselves in Dean Yoltas's office.

"I think you know why you are here."

"Yes," the Trifecta answered in unison.

"Do you care to explain yourselves? Westford has brought forth serious allegations against you."

"No," they answered again in unison.

Dean Yoltas had started her inquiry with the Trifecta hoping to nip the issue in the bud. It did not look as though that would be the case. She dismissed them and asked her secretary to summon three more students asking them to explain themselves. Separately, each took out their phones and played the last lecture of Westford and the class where she had stormed out.

She asked her secretary to summon Gloria.

"Dr. Westford, welcome. Please be seated," Dean Yoltas said before cutting to the chase. "The allegations against the class demand action if you wish to proceed."

"Of course, I want . . ."

Dean Yoltas cut Westford off before continuing. "But I am not sure you want to. As I said, the allegations are serious but I will caution you. The board will do a thorough job of looking into this matter. If you proceed, you may find yourself at the receiving end of the board."

"I stand by my work. They are nothing but selfish entitled children who are trying to make a mockery out of our school and of me. I will not tolerate it. Do you hear me? I want these miscreants expelled." With that, Westford stood resolutely and exited the office.

Dean Yoltas had taken the students' hint. She swiped her phone and would let the cards fall where they may.

CHAPTER 46

Sometimes people have the tendency to cause their own undoing as was the case with Westford. Before the board was convened, a student uploaded the recording online with a video explaining her rant. The video went viral and students and supporters globally asked for her immediate resignation with such furor that her only option was to resign. Her ego had gotten the best of her and the result for her was catastrophic.

"Bummer about Westford," chuckled Rachel as the Trifecta got to work in the second story study room of the library overlooking the quad.

"Yeah, bummer," agreed Charlie.

"Couldn't have happened to a better person," quipped Sally.

"Well, shall we get to work? Anyone have a topic?" asked Rachel.

"How about Cancel Culture? Seems timely," responded Sally and for the next few moments they laughed. With Styles being sick and the stress Westford had caused, they needed a break. The flood gates had been opened.

When they regained their composure, Charlie set a timer on his phone for ten minutes and said, "all right, let's get to it."

With notebooks and pens at their side, they typed and searched and explored. When the alarm sounded, Sally was the first to speak.

"I think Cancel Culture is society's way to bring back fairness. I am not sure it does so and certainly doesn't feel fair to the canceled, but the idea that justice can still prevail no matter someone's pedigree or wealth is important," Sally offered.

"Yeah, so often the rich literally get away with murder and mayhem by dropping cash wherever they can including in the media to paint a muddy picture of the facts," responded Charlie.

"Do you remember that actor? I always thought he was a B actor. The one who killed his camera woman and then tried to say the gun just went off. If that were me, I would be frantic. His first response was a call to his lawyer," said Rachel.

"Exactly, at the elite level they are trained to cast shade," agreed Sally. "In sport there is always someone cheating and doping. We all know that. But in the 90s and 00s there was a doper named Lance Armstrong who built his career on the back of the fable that he didn't dope and then spent much of his fortune to rewrite the narrative in his favor after he was caught. I just learned that he had sued people for defamation who were telling the truth. That's a crime against the system in and of itself."

"Some seem to use it too often. Cancel on. They do so without understanding the effects it may cause. Similar to bullying. The bully is haveing great fun, but how many suicides are caused by being bullied. We will never know. Yet, Cancel Culture does seem like the layman's tool to achieve fairness now and no matter what the system is, some will always be unfairly punished or fall between the cracks. Cancel Culture at least goes after All no matter their zip code or celebrity status," responded Charlie.

"And today, justice was delivered," added Rachel.

They worked for another hour or so on homework and upcoming projects that they had due for other classes using each other as sounding boards for help when needed.

"I just got a message from a group in class that they are meeting up for drinks at the AU pub, the Border. Are you two interested?" asked Rachel.

"Sounds perfect," answered Charlie.

"Let's go," said Sally.

They powered down their computers and headed out to the bar. All's well that ends well.

CHAPTER 47

Styles heard the news of Westford's demise and felt, not the sympathy of a fellow educator who got caught up in a shit show, but of someone who brought the walls crumbling down from the inside out. He hoped that she would get the help she needed or to find the ability to learn from her mistakes yet he doubted both. Misery loves company, and like attracts like. Meaning many searching for help only find themselves in front of those with the same problems and their lives just continue on repeat.

Then he wiped Westford from his mind, took a hot shower, ate breakfast and got ready to walk to school for the first time in weeks. When he opened the door, he found Osa sitting on his stoop ready to walk him to work like a child on his or her first day of school.

"I thought I might walk with you this morning. It is a special one," Osa said.

"I will not say I was expecting this but I will also not say I am surprised."

They laughed together and then headed down the steps of his home and out onto the sidewalk, turning right on their way to AU.

"Can I ask you a question?"

"Yes. Of course. And for the millionth time, stop asking me to ask."

"Stop asking me to stop asking you to ask. It is in my nature."

They laughed again. They were friends.

"What makes those three students so special to you?"

"Very much like you and your brother, I see something special in them and enjoy the voyeuristic pleasure that one gets in watching others succeed. It is the same way I have always felt about Owusa from the day I spent watching him fix my bike, welcome me to your village and share his experiences about life in Ghana and then his life in Ghana as a young gay man with a deep desire to get out. Your brother has succeeded by all measures and when I get down, like we all do, I remember that part of his success is also mine. We are not alone even in our moments of despair."

He paused briefly just to catch his breath. The meds had taken a toll even though he was on the mend.

"Did you have the same pleasure watching me? You've known me for the better part of my life."

"With you, it's a bit more complicated, Osa. When I met you in Ghana, you were a skinny bucktooth big eyed child who spent the time I was with you staring at me but afraid to interact or speak. Your brother and I would laugh about you. When you arrived in the US to your brothers waiting arms, you were no longer a bucktooth big eyed child, you were beginning to become a young woman. And that young woman has blossomed into one of the kindest and caring people I have ever met. Kind beyond measure. A natural caregiver. In ten years, I don't think I have ever seen you put yourself first."

They walked in silence for quite some time before Osa spoke.

"Professor Styles, my culture is different from yours. I am not an American woman. I am someone who is sometimes confused about my cultural identity because I know I will never go back. And you are not a Ghanian man but you are also not a true American man. In my culture men act and women follow or are lead."

"I think I must be missing something. These things I know but it is a strange topic for an early morning walk to work."

"Professor Marc Styles, I have always wanted you to act and you never have. So I have patiently waited. The last few weeks have shown me how I would feel if you were gone. I am from Ghana but I am also a western woman."

She took his hand in hers.

Styles felt the warmth and the love and the jolt of sexual tension the moment their hands connected.

"In my culture, it is popular for men to marry their friends' sisters. This way they are brothers."

Styles squeezed Osa's hand back ever so slightly and she squeezed back. They continued their walk to AU with the smell of blooming cherry blossoms and a symphony of birds. The last few weeks had been hard. The future looked brighter.

The moment Osa left, Styles reached for his phone and dialed Owusa.

"Hello. This is Dr. Owusa. How may I help you?" he answered in his formal tone.

"It's me. Styles."

"Ah. I thought you might call this morning."

"And why is that?"

"A little birdie told me something it was going to do might warrant a call. I think this is the appropriate idiom."

"Then you know why I am calling."

"Frankly speaking, I am very surprised that it has taken this long."

"The call? Now, I am confused."

Styles felt somehow like he was on his back foot. The conversation was not going how he had planned it in his head.

"Why were you expecting this call? What did you think I would say?"

"Styles. You are a smart man but not as much of a man of the world or so it seems. My sister has been in love with you since the day you arrived in Ghana and she was a silent awkward skinny bucktooth big eyed teen. She confided in me then just that. When she came to America, her dream had not changed."

"Why didn't you ever bring it up?"

"Professor, your first lesson to me oh so many years ago was that life unfolds as it should not how we expect it. That it is better to swim with the current of life than against it. I knew that the right time would arrive and it has. How splendid, brother."

They spent the next few minutes laughing and quipping at each other like only brothers can do.

CHAPTER 48

"The haves and have nots will be where we focus our energies today. Many years ago, I was young like you and I milked that time for what it was worth to build a life of experience, not wealth, believing that hard work and diligence and being kind would always provide the wealth I needed to survive. Luckily, it has."

Today marked the first class that Styles was back at the helm. Normally peppy and constantly on the move, he was walking slower and with a cane and moving like someone who had run their first marathon the day before. He ached and some moves gave him a jolt of pain but he was back where he wanted to be in the classroom.

"I remember one such day. I had landed in India. Now, I understand that health and wealth are relative. You define both based on your surroundings and your experiences. Your brains are actively working on the problem now. The top is easier to define. There are simply fewer of them and they have more. Anyone driving a Ferrari or sailing a yacht is wealthy. But where is the line that separates the two groups? That is what I want you to define.

"Back to India and I remember this moment as clearly as day. I was in the Indian city of Hyderabad about two blocks from my hotel. Ahead of me was an overpass with electrical wiring that would make any OSHA official cringe. Nothing in my view looked clean or new. It all looked old and well used. The city was bustling.

"I was in a tuk tuk that I had hired for the day. The driver was a man about 30 who had a wife and three kids. He was a chipper nice guy. We were sitting at a traffic light of a six lane highway in the middle of the city. We were on the left side in the farthest left lane. It is a right-hand drive country. His tuk tuk was well taken care of but still old and well-used. To his right was a nondescript Toyota sedan taxi that literally exists all over Asia like confetti. To its right in the far right lane was a red Ferrari and behind it, a bus. Now, in the western world, if a bus fits 45 passengers and one driver then a full bus carries 46 souls. In the rest of the world a bus carries the driver plus one more. There were men sitting on the roof, some hanging off the back and others sitting halfway in and halfway out of the windows. This was my view from the far left to the center median.

To my left was the emergency lane which housed a plethora of pedestrians and cyclists and to my delight and surprise, an elephant and its rider. 'Toto, we are not in Kansas anymore was all I could think' at this visual cacophony and what it represented.

After my trip to India, I spent some time in Yangon, Myanmar where I would run in the back neighborhoods that housed only locals and chased wide-eyed children through their living rooms to the delight of them and their families. In those neighborhoods, I was the red Ferrari. It would be the equivalent if your favorite athlete or celebrity walked into your home and made themselves a coffee.

During my time there which was about two years, I lived in an apartment across from the school I worked at and would regularly clean out my wardrobe giving my clothes to the security guards and cleaning staff. By the time I left, I came to realize that my discards were there after work clothes and that their uniforms, for most, was all the clothing they had."

Styles said all of this while sitting on a stool next to the desk on the stage in the lecture hall. When he was done, the class could see that his energy was drained but his eyes were sharp and alert and ready for action.

"At that traffic light and running through those back neighborhoods, I came to realize that the rest of the world defines wealth as happiness, health and a full belly. The western world's traditional greeting is related to the time of day. Good morning. Good afternoon. In Myanmar, their traditional greeting is 'Tamin sah byee byee lah?' which translates to 'Have you eaten your rice today?', and the expectation is that if the answer is no, you will help. Money certainly affords us more food and better access to health but it doesn't assure us joy.

"My question that you are tasked with today is to explore and create a system in which the pedestrian, the cyclist, the camel rider, the tuktuk passenger, the taxi driver, the locals and the red Ferrari driver can exist without any having the urge desire to harm each other or the ability to ignore those that need help. Are there any questions?"

The class was quiet and subdued. They were happy to have Styles back at the helm and didn't want to tax him by asking many questions as their way of saying they were happy to have him back. They had seen the alternative.

"Good luck. I look forward to hearing your answers. Now, get to work!"

CHAPTER 49

"**W**ell, we are clearly haves or on the path to being haves. All of us here at AU, even those on full scholarship. Education is a clear divider, especially a liberal one that teaches thinking," stated Rachel.

"Sure but there certainly seems to be a lot of degree holding baristas with student debt slinging coffee," responded Charlie.

"Being given a gift or a tool doesn't mean you will succeed. It just means you have a higher likelihood to do so. Many heirs of the wealthy go broke and wind up penniless. Noone succeeds by resting on their laurels. I remember hearing a story at a training camp in Boulder, Colorado. I must have been 13 or 14 but it stuck."

Sally was a star runner without an ego. She let her hard work and legs do the talking and it was rare for her to flex herself as an athlete. When she did, Rachel and Charlie came to realize Sally usually offered a gem.

She told the story about the coach in Boulder. The coach had asked the athletes who the best basketball player ever was which led to the normal debate between Kobe Bryant, LeBron James and Michael Jordan. The coach stoked the fire just to make his point. When sides had been taken and right before blows may have erupted, the coach quieted down the auditorium.

'Bryant, James and Jordan only represent the best basketball players in the NBA. The best basketball player fell through the cracks. The sad part is that they probably know it. As did the best coach, teacher, lawyer, doctor, actor and musician. Talent does not even ensure that you will get through the door. Remember, Jordan was cut from his basketball team and Messi was told he was too small to play football.

Look around you. Some of you will win. Some of you will spend your whole career chasing your first win. Some, outside this room, will never make it to their first starting line or whistle blow. Those who succeed do so because those around them have the tools and the desire to help. Success does not manifest or grow by itself. It needs fuel like all living things. The best basketball player of all time was told they weren't good enough to play ball and to find another pursuit. Once they gained wisdom and the window closed, then they understood the mistakes that were made. I imagine their lives to be difficult. I bestow you this story as fuel to succeed. You are winners.'

And then he was done. He walked off stage and the rest of the training camp was about work. Two runs a day followed by stretching, core work and recovery and of course, lots of fuel.

"I remember this guy. This coach. Because of what he said. Haves are lucky. The stars are aligned for them and for us. I am sure we are Haves now but that does not mean we will be a Have in our future," Sally went on to say.

Both Charlie and Rachel nodded in agreement and all three were glad to be back in the second floor study room of the library overlooking the quad thinking about and trying to uncover the truths to the questions Styles had posited who had returned that day to the lectern to a class full of 'too cool for school smiles'.

CHAPTER 50

Spring was in full swing. Birds chirped. Buds bloomed. The quad became a fury of activity with some sunbathing, some reading and studying and others just plain hanging out. At the corner by the big weeping willow tree stood Donald and making his way through the quad was Ted. They were handing out flyers for an upcoming climbing trip and looking for interested students.

Across the quad out of the corner of his eye Donald caught a glimpse of something familiar but still out of focus. A memory of sorts. Then the memory became clear. His parents were crossing the quad beelining it for the weeping willow and now, the young man in front of it.

"We would like to see Dean Yoltas," stated Mr. Abbott to the Dean's secretary.

"Let me check to see if he is available. Might I know what this is concerning?"

"No, you may not," answered Mrs. Abbott.

The Dean's secretary picked up her phone and dialed the dean's extension. They had codes or secret speak between them to help better communicate in front of prying ears. The secretary told the Dean that her two o'clock meeting needed to be postponed and that there were parents waiting to see her.

Dean Yoltas took a few deep breaths. The code translated to make time. Irate parents are here.

After composing herself for a few more moments, Dean Yoltas stood up from her desk, walked to the door, opened it and ushered the Abbotts into her office.

"Please take a seat," she said pointing to the two chairs in front of her desk while moving behind the desk back to her perch.

"Let me get straight to the point. Our son Donald is a student at your school. When he chose this school, it was based on its reputation. A reputation that I question now. Donald graduated at the top of his class. He has never received less than an A on anything. He is smart and athletic, but more importantly, he has a good head on his shoulders. Two weeks ago, he shared with us his report card. There were two Bs. Then, after trying to reach him, we were given the brush off and the cold shoulder. He said he was too busy to talk. If he was too busy to talk, he would not have had Bs. What type of school are you running?"

Yoltas knew of Donald because she had known of Ted and his struggles as a student and as a young gay man. She had seen him beaming a few times and had openly asked him about the cause.

"Ted, you seem happier than normal."

Ted smiled back. "I am. Thanks."

"Might I inquire as to why?"

"Yeah. Sure. I met someone. I like him. He likes me. And he now climbs too." and with that, Ted was off.

So it was no surprise that through the grapevine when she learned that Ted was dating a young man named Donald. She had yet to meet him, but as any good educator, had looked into who he was and had taken a glance at his file. Dean Yoltas was not surprised to see his parents sitting across from him glaring at her.

"We sent our son to this school based on its academic reputation, now he is failing," said Mrs. Abbott.

"I assure you that he is not failing. Bs are not Fs and are not the gateway to Fs. They are a sign that he is succeeding in school but faltering or struggling somewhere else in his life. I have been an educator for most of my life. When good students have dips," Dean Yoltas made the hand gesture of a wave, "it is normal. Life has both ups and downs. Usually the dips head to higher peaks." She smiled inwardly at her own irony.

"But . . .," Mr. Abbott started before he had collected his thoughts and then continued, "he and his wife had never brushed us off before or had never been without contact with their son for more than a day or two. We are afraid. Is it drugs?"

"We see on the news about America's drug problem all the time," chimed in Mrs Abbott. "We just never thought it would happen to our Donald. What should we do?"

Dean Yoltas responded carefully, "I would recommend you to start by finding your son and having a conversation with him. Ask him frankly about the drugs to put your minds at ease and after you speak with him, my door is open if you want to further our discussion."

With that, Dean Yoltas ushered Donald's parents out of her office and asked her secretary to look up Donald's schedule.

The secretary responded that Donald had the afternoon free but one more class in the evening at 7pm.

"If he is on campus, I would head across the quad to the big weeping willow tree. There is a stone walkway that leads to our outdoor program. Some students like to hang out there and on a day like this, if you don't see him in the quad, he may be there."

The Abbotts left the office of the Dean and headed down the

stairs and out the back entrance to the quad where they saw the big weeping willow across a green sea of students.

CHAPTER 51

"**A**re you sure we should be here?" asked Mrs. Abbott.

"Yes. If Donald is in trouble, we should help him to nip the problem in the bud."

As they made their way across the quad, Mrs. Abbott saw a vague shape she recognized as her son. As the shape came into focus, she started to think the worst.

"Do you see him? Oh God. He is so thin. It must be drugs. Look at him. He's so skinny," Mrs. Abbott said in a panic to her husband.

"We'll get to the bottom of this right now," Mr. Abbottr answered.

Across the quad, the shapes came into focus. Donald could see the silhouettes of his parents making their way directly towards him. He took a deep breath like the ones he was trained to do when making a hard move on the wall and started to walk towards them.

"Hi Mom. Hi Dad," Donald said as they approached. "What brings you to campus?"

Mrs. Abbott hugged her son and then pulled back weeping.

"Your mother thinks you are on drugs. Are you?" Mr. Abbott asked.

Donald laughed and then regained his composure.

"No. Nope. No drugs." Donald put 2+2 together. "I started rock climbing a few months ago. I think I told you and leaned up."

"No, you are sick," Mrs. Abbott blurted out.

"No, I am not. I am actually doing really well. Probably the best I have ever done in fact."

"Then why did you get Bs?"

"Yeah. That. I've been meaning to talk to you about that. Let's go sit down."

"Oh no. I knew it was something horrible. He's asking us to sit down. Oh god, I need to sit down," said Mrs. Abbott.

There was a picnic table with two students that Donald knew sitting at it. He walked over and asked them if he could use the space to talk to his parents. They agreed and left, and the three sat down.

"Mom. Dad. You guys love me. I know that. At the beginning of the school year, I was struggling. I had my first failure. I got a bad grade. I talked to the teacher and worked through it but could only bring it back up to a B. It was fair but that initial B had a snowball effect. I got into a funk and missed handing in a big assignment."

"So you are not okay?" Mr. Abbott asked.

"We are here for you. We will help you. What can we do?" Mrs. Abbott asked.

"I am not finished. When I got here, I had only known success and popularity. I thought those things would follow me here and in the beginning they did. Then that well dried up."

"Are you lonely?" asked Mrs. Abbott, interrupting. "What can we do to help?"

"Let him finish," snapped Mr. Abbott. "It's obvious the boy has something else to say.

As Donald collected his thoughts, he saw Ted watching in the distance.

"Whew. All right. Here it goes. The teacher that gave me a B I didn't like. I thought he didn't like me," with Mrs. Abbott biting her lip, Donald continued. "This teacher saw that I was struggling. I thought he didn't like me but in fact, it turns out, it was only me who didn't like him. He could see that I was struggling and reached out to help. He spoke with me and introduced me to the outdoor program."

Donald pointed behind him past the weeping willow down the stone walkway to the door with the little sign hanging above. I guess he thought I needed to explore some new things. He was right. One of the things I tried was rock climbing. I fell in love with it and have been climbing almost daily ever since. It's awesome."

Donald blew out a big breath of air before continuing.

"And I fell in love. My grades are back up. All As." Donald continued, "I am fitter and stronger than I have ever been. I am a better version of myself than I was at the beginning of the year. Ironically, I credit Professor Styles, the teacher I didn't like. I am doing great."

Mrs. Abbott's mood shifted from fear to joy. She could see that sitting across from her was the young man she had raised coming into his own. He was no longer her boy but her son who was now a man.

Mr. Abbott knew there was a catch. He was not yet relieved. He could see that there was something else lingering out there.

"So? When do we get to meet the lucky lady?" asked Mrs. Abbott..

"Mmm. You don't."

Mr. Abbott knew now what was coming and chuckled when Mrs. Abbott asked, "Why not? Does she not live close by?"

Donald searched the eyes of his parents and saw that his mother was genuinely confused and that his father had already done the math and accepted what was about to come, and eyed him hoping for help.

"No, dear, that's not what he's saying."

Mrs. Abbott looked at her husband, still confused.

"We are not going to meet her. We are going to meet him and I imagine by Donald's sly hand gestures, nods and where he has been glancing since we sat down, it's probably the man standing behind you to your right squeezing a roll of flyers in his hands like he is wringing out a wet dish towel. Just a guess though."

Mrs. Abbott looked over her shoulder at the unkempt mop of hair on a beanpole body and saw what her son must have seen. A young man deserving of love. She beamed and welcomed Ted to the table without hesitation as a new addition to her family.

"I'm Doloros and this is my husband Walter," Doloros said with an outstretched hand.

"I'm Ted. Nice to meet you. Donald has told me a lot about you. He says that you like to quilt in your spare time?"

"A charmer. Better watch this one Donald or he may slip away."

They all laughed and immediately the mood shifted from tense to jovial.

"We were about to go climbing? Do you want to join?" asked Ted.

"Today has been a day of firsts so I don't see why not," replied Walter.

The rest of the afternoon was spent in the climbing gym.

"On belay," Doloros said.

"Belay is on," Walter responded.

"Climbing."

"Climb on."

CHAPTER 52

"I thought this was going to go very differently," Donald said at dinner that night.

The four were eating at a small Italian restaurant with red and white check tablecloths and Italian memorabilia strewn on shelves around the place. It smelled of oregano, wine and steaming pasta. Students, faculty and locals alike enjoyed eating there when they could.

"Why is that?" asked his mom. "I thought you knew that we loved you."

"I don't know. I guess I was just worried. I've heard stories."

"My parents disowned me," piped in Ted. "Maybe, we were going off of that."

The food arrived and they dug in.

With a clump of tomato on his beard and a straggler piece of spaghetti making its way into his mouth, Walter spoke, "When we got together, I remember this as clear as day now, your mom, Doloros, said to me that we were going to work through a book. I was love struck so I agreed."

"I remember that. The book of questions that Liz gave us."

"Yep. It asked all sorts of weird questions to me. How do you feel about holidays? Describe your parenting style? Crap like that. It didn't seem important at the time. But as time went by, I realized it came to save our marriage a couple of times. Like many families, they were silent on big issues. *Gay* was a word spoken in whispers."

"Mine too. You were taught to be one way as though no other options existed. Well, here it is. Your son is gay," Ted interrupted.

They all laughed before Walter returned to speaking and the rest returned to eating and listening.

"That book forced us to ask hard questions and solve problems before they arose and has helped us to stay together for 25+ years. We knew each other before we were married and when issues arose, we knew how each other would respond and acted accordingly. If I was a rich man, I'd send this book out to every young couple. Anyway, one question was 'how would you react if you child was gay?' I had never given it a thought. I assumed it would happen to other people's kids. Not mine."

"That was doozy. We did not see eye to eye," stated Doloros.

"Why?" asked Donald. "And why is this the first time I am hearing about this?"

"Two reasons. One, out of site, out of mind. Most of the questions were directed to early issues that people experience in marriage. The second, I don't think any parent wants gay children. I think good parents accept and love gay children. There is a difference. No parent wants their kids to have hardship," said Walter.

"That night, that's where we arrived. We decided that we would accept and love a gay child no matter what," said Doloros.

"Sounds like a good book," said Ted.

"We love you son despite your Bs and your choice of sports. By the way, I am having a hard time with this spoon. I don't think my arms have been this sore since I can't remember when," chided Walter.

"Oh, I am so glad it's not just me," Doloros answered before grabbing her husband's elbow in a hold, leaning into his and giving him a big kiss on the cheek. "My hero."

The rest of the dinner was spent laughing and reminiscing about the day on the wall climbing and by the time dinner was over, Ted had been welcomed into the family.

"I am so proud that I made it to the top," Walter said.

"Climbing isn't only about strength. It's about using what you have. Women are better at it as a whole. You have a higher strength to weight ratio and a better sense of reason. Women think before they act more than men," Ted explained.

"Well, I am a fan. I hope there is a gym near us at home," Doloros said.

"Yeah, it would be fun and maybe we could come out here in the fall and try climbing on the rocks with you two," Walter said in agreement.

"Invitation accepted," responded Donald. "Sounds great. Truth is I've kinda missed you since climbing and coming out."

Donald's parents left for the evening and headed to a hotel for the night. Ted and Donald walked home happy as two young lovers accepted by their families can be.

"I want you to know something now. No matter what happens between us, I want you to know that my parents will be there for you too."

Ted stopped walking and with a calloused hand took the elbow of Donald and kissed his cheek before saying, "I know."

CHAPTER 53

Class was in session. Styles was at the lectern.

"Over the course of the year, we have explored many topics asking questions about the rules or dogma attached to them. What we have found is that many traditions and cultural norms do not pass the scrutiny test yet have survived the test of time. Why is this? What causes this phenomenon? Why is it that even though all of us who can see the flaws and know that evolution exists at some level, do some spend their lives fighting it every twist and turn? The bicycle is a more efficient form of transportation than our feet. Our cell phones communicate better than any form before, especially against fires from high point to high point. Medicine has advanced to the point that we survive many complicated procedures instead of dying on the table because the leeches or the bleeding didn't cure us of the sicknesses and in fact, were never truly cures for our ailments.

"But here we are, in a time in which we can literally fly to the moon and someday will fly to Mars yet are willing to fight over the smallest changes to our traditions and cultural norms that have been programmed into us. If we apply the concept of AU and Neplanta, the borderlands, I think we would find that without the ability to adapt and change, we would perish and those that Gloria Anzaldua observed living a dual life on the borderlands were just those who were ahead of the times.

They were born with the ability to adapt. They were never so stuck or rigid in their thinking or ways to believe that the imaginary line, in most cases, that demarks one group from another had any true influence over their lives. The lines were really just there so that those that work at the census bureau or as cartologists could be kept busy, and so that, and this is my voice coming through, those who have had power in their families traditionally can carry on the tradition of maintaining and reaping the benefits of that power."

Styles stopped. He sipped a glass of water and sat down on the stool to the right of the lectern at the bottom of the lecture hall.

"Your final assignment is to solve man's riddle. How do we get the horse to drink water? In other words, how do we get others to actually change? Your task for the next class and as your final is to create a solution. Now, are there any questions?"

The class was quiet but energized. The students had their hooks into ideas and Styles could see their wheels were spinning. He quietly left the room giving the students the remainder of the class time to work.

That evening, Charlie, Sally and Rachel met in the top right corner study room of the library overlooking the quad and got to work. Charlie set the phone in the center of the table after setting the alarm.

When the alarm buzzed, Rachel was the first to speak, "Why is change so difficult for so many?"

"That seems like the age old question," responded Charlie.

"It shouldn't. It should be the opposite but I think I have a clue," Sally said.

What connected the Trifecta was not just their similarities but their differences. Over the first few weeks together, they had laid some foundation. Just because someone was right, it didn't mean that the other person was wrong. They came to realize that sometimes all were wrong or all were right depending on the case. And when arguments started to erupt, they were able to nip them in the bud putting their differences aside for their shared desire to find deeper truths believing that there is right and wrong.

Charlie looked at the world through the lens of a bohemian. He was a natural shape shifter or border crosser. He was hard wired to fit into any grouping or situation with ease but found it hard to take root. Rachel was a brilliant strong stubborn feminist. That she put up with Charlie said more about Charlie's ability to fit in than hers to accept others. Sally was an elite athlete. She viewed her world through sport and taking actions to win and saw the fruits of her labor as she rose through the national and global rankings.

"Maybe it has to do with age. I started down the road of endurance athletes like I normally do and then broadened the scope to all athletes. Then I started to see my hypothesis in action everywhere. The data is there. We peak and then we are finished. We hope that our peak happens when we are at the top. Some bow out gracefully. Stories are written and then they fade away as new stars rise and come into view. But, there is also animosity towards those rising stars that are nipping at our heels. We see them. Some mentor and help them and others do everything in their power to stand in their way,"

"Yeah, it's like some are afraid to hand over the torch," Charlie interrupted.

"Exactly," Sally responded.

"Think about Botox and hair plugs. They identify those people. Those unwilling, I guess ultimately, to accept life on life's terms. Aging is part of life," Rachel added.

"And when those people are in power, there's the problem. They are unwilling to give it up because of a deep hard-wired fear of change. They don't want to sit on the sidelines and watch the next generation surpass them. It goes against their evolutionary desire to survive," Sally stated.

Over the next hour they continued down this vein of thinking and arrived at a destination that offered a solution while clearly identifying the problem. They came to understand that the problem was deep and the solution landed in the hands of all. More often than not, those, like them, with a willingness to adapt and change to meet their surroundings, did so at the cost of change. Because their thinking was designed to accept life on life's terms, they rarely rocked the boat and therefore all other passengers barely felt the shifts. The problem was that on one side was evolution and on the other tradition and normative thinking designed to enforce the systems that were already in place. To put it bluntly, one side has new knowledge and merit to stand on and the other has legacy and tradition. We see this today. The older worker who does very little to ensure the safety of the newcomers they govern or manage. Governments that are not acting to save our home, Planet Earth, while billions just struggle to keep their personal ship afloat. It's a Catch-22. The youth uncover the answers, as they are designed to do, while the old stop the evolutionary wheel from spinning. Then the young become old and continue the cycle until action needs to be taken or it's too late. A catastrophe upon us or the destruction or extinction of a system or species.

"That was one of our best dialogues but I am exhausted," Charlie complained.

"Same here."

"Call it a night?" asked Sally.

The Trifecta nodded in agreement and turned off the light as they left the top right corner study room of the library overlooking the quad.

CHAPTER 54

The semester was coming to an end and a break was in order. Sally had been awarded a scholarship to go to Kenya for the summer and train with fellow hopeful Olympians.

Charlie, on the other hand, was experiencing a serious case of wanderlust and when Owusa had asked if Charlie was interested in visiting and helping out in his village in Ghana, Charlie's immediate response was yes. By the time the semester was over, his backpack had been waiting by the door for days.

Rachel, meanwhile, had been offered a summer internship in Mt. Hood, Oregon teaching preschoolers English and art. She had wanted the region so had accepted the position without hesitation. She was not a kid person and was secretly scared shitless about the prospect of working with many of them over the summer.

But now it was perfect. They were laying in bed enjoying a lazy finals week morning. Most of their exams had been earlier in the week and now they only had one more to prepare for. Professor Styles and they were not worried.

"Not to be a buzzkill but what happens after this summer and next year?" Rachel asked.

"I was enjoying the moment. Thanks," responded Sally with a

sarcastic tone and an elbow to Rachel's ribs.

"I don't know," said Charlie.

"How would you feel about either Las Vegas rules or just calling it what it is? What happens over summer stays over summer just be careful about bringing back something you or we can't wash off and see where we are in the fall. Call it a break," said Rachel.

They all agreed.

As the semester unwinded, so did their tryst. The work in the study room on the second floor of the library overlooking the quad dwindled to barely a drip. They simply had little work to do and were mentally exhausted so they found themselves spending more time at home.

Rachel buzzed with energy. Always. She had two modes. On. Off. And when the switch was set to off, she did very little.

Charlie was more airy. He swayed with the wind like bamboo. Never too rigid to be afraid of change. Some changes he liked more than others but as a pollyanna, he accepted life on life's terms.

Sally was a goal setter. She planned and executed her plans which had made it so interesting that she was laying naked in bed with two partners both of whom she cared deeply for if not loved.

"I love you two but this doesn't feel permanent. It is right now. It's all that matters if that makes sense."

"Of course it does," said Charlie. "If Styles and this year has taught us anything, it's that the now is all we have."

They all laughed and then hugged and kissed and continued hugging and kissing for quite some time and the morning had faded away.

When they were finished and finally out of bed drinking coffee and eating lunch, Charlie was the first to speak.

"We are together because we are in the period of living in the wind. Ebbing and flowing and finding life. I love both of you now and forever but now is what it is, fleeting."

"I love both of you too. What I have learned from us is to let the now unfold as it should not how I want it to. After summer, no matter what happens, I'll see you in the second floor study room of the library overlooking the quad," said Sally. "I am not willing to give that up."

"Giving that up was never on the table," Rachel jibed. "That was a given. It's just these moments that may change."

"Let's play it by ear. Live. Let live. Be," answered Charlie.

CHAPTER 55

Professor Styles sat at a chair next to the lectern in the lecture hall as the students filed in for the final class of the year. Once most had arrived, Styles began, "A school year is a chunk of time. The younger we are, the more time it represents. Not until we hit thirty or forty do we start to view a year as fleeting and short. In our youth, it is long. So when a school year ends, sometimes it feels like it was a lifetime. Life is like that. It is one of the few things that can turn on a dime. One minute you are headed one way and the next, another.

"College is like that too. Most look back at their college days and can see the fruit of their work. Whether it's the husband or wife or partner sitting across from them sipping coffee, kids somewhere continuing their legacy or the career or path that they have journeyed. College is about exploring the fence to see which side you want to land on.

"Anzaldua University was built on that foundation. The foundation to help students explore themselves so that they would be provided the tools to create and live their best version of themselves. Tradition is where people go who are afraid of change. Traditions are not inherently wrong, but when they stop motion, the tradition's purpose changes. It changes from something that we do out of love and joy to something we do out of obligation and formality. If it's the latter, it stops movement, and movement, change, evolution, innovation and invention are simply the synonyms for the one tool that has helped us survive thus far. The ability to think and adapt to any situation as necessary.

"It has been my great pleasure to have survived this semester so that I could dust off this speech and be here to give it to you as my parting words for the year. I wish you a happy and healthy summer in which you get to take some steps that get you closer to your dreams even if those steps are just a break with a remote and a TV. Thank you for your hard work and diligence and bearing with the class during my absence. Godspeed."

The class started clapping and then stood for Professor Styles as he collected his things, walked up the center aisle and exited the lecture hall.

"I don't think I will ever have a class or teacher that impacts my life like Styles," said Charlie.

"Me neither," responded Rachel.

After Styles left, Donald quickly moved towards the Trifecta.

"Excuse me," Donald said.

"Hey," Sally responded.

"What's up?" asked Rachel.

"I just wanted to say that I got off on the wrong foot with this class, the three of you and this year. I wanted to apologize. It's been pretty cool to see the three of you feed off of each other. I am glad I got to see it."

"We are sorry for the brush off too," responded Sally.

"It's okay. I needed a few kicks. I needed to find out who I really am. The kick helped. Hope to see you next year." And with that Donald left.

"Sometimes I forget that others have challenges too. I think we live in such personal bubbles that we think the world revolves around us and our immediate circle. It's hard to see past that sometimes," said Rachel.

"For sure. It's probably a leftover from when we the universe did revolve around us," Charlie responded.

"Yeah, from when the stars were just pin pricks in the fabric separating us from the heavens. Sometimes it's amazing just how far we have come and just how far we will probably go," responded Sally.

"I have some things to do this morning. Meet at home for dinner at about 5pm?" asked Rachel.

"I'll grab pizzas and beers on the way," Charlie stated.

And just like that, the semester and junior year was over. Remember life is fleeting. Enjoy the now.

CHAPTER 56

After summer break, the Trifecta were inseparable. Different classes, different majors but at night, most of the time, they could be found in the second story study room of the library overlooking the quad. The nights that they weren't together, they were exploring the world or each other with almost a scientific approach of the latter.

When they graduated, Sally packed her bags and headed to Colorado Springs, Colorado. She had qualified for the Boston Marathon and the Olympics and was the reigning Collegiate National Champion in the half marathon. Her life was cut out for her for the foreseeable future.

Charlie was sitting on her bed watching her back up the last of her things. She was headed out in the morning bright and early and Charlie was giving her a ride to the airport.

"You know, you could meet me in Colorado Springs?"

"I know, but my compass is pointing south and I am going to follow it. I'll spend the day tomorrow selling my car and buying a ticket to Portland to visit Rachel and go south from there to the border. I've always wanted to see Central and South America."

"I figured as much. Just a bit sad that whatever this was is ending."

"Never know what the future holds."

Sally went on to be an Olympic Champion. She met her husband Luigi in the Olympic Village of Beijing and they hit it off almost immediately. He was a champion swimmer from just outside of Lake Como, Italy where she moved to live after the Olympics.

The week before Rachel had been offered her dream job, helping women who have been abused get off their feet and move forward. It was a grassroots program that helped to re-educate their clients so that they had all the needed tools to survive on their own. She had been elated by the offer and had not hesitated in accepting the position which had started the Monday after graduation.

"Hey stranger. Thanks for picking me up," Charlie said as he arrived in Portland.

"Pleasure. Sorry for the gray weather. It was sunny yesterday. Let's get a coffee before heading to my house."

They hugged and exchanged pleasantries and talked about life.

"I have to be honest with you Charlie. I am really excited. I met someone and she is the cat's meow."

"Cat's meow," Charlie laughed. "She must be something. Do I get the pleasure of meeting her?"

"Yes. She's at home now. It's been a whirlwind and I wanted your reaction before dropping it on you."

"Rachel, I love you like I love Sally, as an ex that I hope to always be friends with. Nothing more, hopefully nothing less. That's the plain and simple of it."

"Pals forever," Rachel answered. "How's Sally?"

"She's great. I saw her to the airport this morning and she is off on the adventure of a future Olympian. How cool is that to be part of her story? Awesome."

The night went as expected. Charlie was introduced to Beatrice and could see immediately that the two were perfect together. He stayed for the weekend and was dropped off at the bus terminal on Rachel's way to work. They had Charlie promise he would keep in touch. He knew he would.

Charlie's life path was different. He learned for learning's sake and played for playing's sake. So while he was as gifted intellectually as Rachel and maybe, with training, as fit as Sally, he had no doors open to him with the exception of his desire to live his own life and write his own story.

And with that, the trifecta dissolved and the second floor study room of the library overlooking the quad became a distant memory while the three, each in their own right, used the threads they had collected along the way to stitch their own life quilts.

AFTERWORD

At the core, I am an educator who believes that the job of an educator is to guide, to show, not tell. Pulling Threads aimed to be just that. A simple book that provided the sketch or framework for the reader so that you could fill in the blanks and create a mental picture in your mind.

Pulling Threads tells the story of how students and educators work through the world of school and that not all life is doom and gloom. Sometimes our dreams are waiting just around the corner; we just can't see it yet.

All over the world, we are bombarded with bad news. From experience, after the storm there usually is calm. Weathering the storm is the challenge, but one that we can survive if we work together. Society is fractured because there are too many walls up all around us. Maybe, we should think about tearing some down.

If you are interested in learning more about the author, Dylan can be contacted at horizoncoaching.org or at linguisticscoaching@gmail.com.

www.ingramcontent.com/pod-product-compliance
Lightning Source LLC
Chambersburg PA
CBHW061510120726

48001CB00004B/1278